La PETITE FOUR

Regina Scott

razOr
bill

La Petite Four

RAZORBILL

Published by the Penguin Group
Penguin Young Readers Group
345 Hudson Street, New York, New York 10014, U.S.A.
Penguin Group (USA) Inc., 375 Hudson Street, New York, New York 10014, U.S.A.
Penguin Group (Canada), 90 Eglinton Avenue East, Suite 700, Toronto,
Ontario, Canada M4P 2Y3 (a division of Pearson Penguin Canada Inc.)
Penguin Books Ltd, 80 Strand, London WC2R 0RL, England
Penguin Ireland, 25 St Stephen's Green, Dublin 2, Ireland
(a division of Penguin Books Ltd)
Penguin Group (Australia), 250 Camberwell Road, Camberwell,
Victoria 3124, Australia (a division of Pearson Australia Group Pty Ltd)
Penguin Books India Pvt Ltd, 11 Community Centre, Panchsheel Park,
New Delhi – 110 017, India
Penguin Group (NZ), 67 Apollo Drive, Rosedale, North Shore 0632, New Zealand
(a division of Pearson New Zealand Ltd.)
Penguin Books (South Africa) (Pty) Ltd, 24 Sturdee Avenue,
Rosebank, Johannesburg 2196, South Africa

Penguin Books Ltd, Registered Offices: 80 Strand, London WC2R 0RL, England

10 9 8 7 6 5 4 3 2 1

Library of Congress Cataloging-in-Publication Data is available

Printed in the United States of America

La
PETITE
FOUR

To the Lord, for inspiration and encouragement
To my Emily and my Larry, for believing in me
To Jessica and Lexa for working so hard
To the ever-supportive Kris for brainstorming, Lord Snedley,
and blood pooling about decapitated bodies
And to library staff everywhere, especially Marsha Bates
of the Mid-Columbia Library and John Charles of the
Scottsdale Public Library, who point us to books that teach,
enrich, and set us to dreaming of all we can be

✤ 1 ✤

To London at Last

Lady Emily Southwell, trained from birth to be the refined daughter of a duke, did the unthinkable. She hoisted the soft blue of her skirts, slipped out of the Barnsley School Grand Salon to leave the remaining seven members of the graduating class to their celebration, and ran. The sounds of their laughter echoed behind her, calling her to return, to accept their well wishes, to accept her dismal future.

She refused. She would not let them witness the depths of her vast disappointment.

And she could not let Lord Robert find her.

She dashed down the school's main corridor, the slap of her amethyst-colored satin slippers against the polished floor nearly as loud as the gasp of her breath. Paneled doorways and soaring arches whipped past. Paintings of sweeping landscapes and dark myths framed in heavy gilt were little more than a blur, even Miss Martingale's favorite, *The Fall of Man*.

A rather inferior piece, really. Emily could do better.

A voice cried behind her, calling her name. Emily didn't dare turn to see who it was. As long as she pretended she didn't know her fate was waiting downstairs, she was free.

She rounded the corner, flew up the short flight of marble

stairs, and ducked into the sunny bedchamber she'd shared the last few years with her three dearest friends, Priscilla Tate and Daphne and Ariadne Courdebas. The sounds of the elegant soiree faded away, but Miss Martingale's terrible announcement still rang in Emily's ears.

How could it have come to this? They had waited *years* for this day, when they completed their education at the Barnsley School for Young Ladies and went to London. The old brick building had never looked so festive, adorned with laurel wreaths, gold-trimmed draperies, and banners welcoming their distinguished guests. All eight members of the graduating class had been equally adorned in their best silks, as bright as the tulips planted along the drive.

Except for Emily, of course. She'd worn dark blue.

Then, in what should have been Emily's proudest moment, their headmistress had announced the winner of the Prize in Art, a prize Emily had longed for since her first day at the esteemed school. How could she have lost, and to *Acantha Dalrymple* of all people?!

She yanked the white satin sash off her shoulder. What did graduation matter if she was not acknowledged? Who cared for congratulations, spiced punch and cakes, fond remembrances of the past eight years, when her future was entirely blighted?

Or would be, if she didn't leave. Now.

Her green wool traveling gown lay spread on the four-poster bed, but no maid stood ready to help. They were all downstairs, working at the celebration for the parents and well-wishers. It was all up to her, then. She reached behind her and tugged at the tapes that held her gown shut, fingers slipping on the soft material. Oh, why did everything have to be difficult!

"Here, let me," Daphne said, hurrying into the room. Her breath came easily, unlike Emily's, and not a honey-colored hair was out of place. Emily had once painted her as Artemis, goddess of the hunt, all rousing good cheer. Daphne's mother had taken exception to the diaphanous robes and insisted that Emily paint on a high-necked bombazine gown instead. Who ever heard of Artemis riding to the hunt in bombazine?

But Daphne did not seem to appreciate her height and athletic abilities. To ensure a successful Season, she'd turned to etiquette books the last few weeks before graduation and memorized Lord Pompadour Snedley's *Guide to London's Beau Monde*, illustrated and annotated.

Emily turned and felt Daphne's strong fingers make quick work of the troublesome tapes. "Priscilla is speaking to her father," her friend reported as she worked, "and Ariadne will be along shortly. What more do you need?"

"My half boots," Emily replied, kicking off her slippers as she shrugged out of the muslin. "And where is my travel case?"

"I'll find it," the younger Ariadne volunteered as she entered in a rush of pale pink skirts, breath a gasp, darker curls wilting around her face. Though she and Daphne were only eleven months apart, they had little in common in looks or abilities other than a kind temperament and Emily's friendship. In fact, Ariadne always reminded Emily of a canary—small, round, bright, and inquisitive—just the sort of encouragement one needed on a rainy day.

Or when one's life had ended before it had begun.

Daphne slipped the traveling gown over Emily's head. The warm folds slid down her body, but still she felt chilled. As the wool settled around her, she plucked out her locket from the top of her chemise and laid the gold oval on the wool, the familiar touch steadying her.

Emily peered into the dressing table mirror long enough to run her fingers through her hair. Not that it mattered. Her black hair was more frizzy than curly, and the frizz was always worse in the rain. They had a lot of rain in England. And her features were too angular for her to be called beautiful. She'd seen too many portraits to think otherwise.

"It truly is unfair," Daphne said as she came to finish the fastenings. "You should have won the prize."

Emily took one look at Daphne's warm smile in the mirror and felt her eyes grow hot and scratchy. Yes, she should have won; she'd done everything to win the Barnsley Prize in Art. But crying wouldn't help. She'd cried enough when her mother had died eight years ago; it hadn't brought her mother back. Besides, Emily would much rather solve a problem than cry over it.

Which was why she had to get to London and see her father— His Grace, the Duke of Emerson.

"Your valise," Ariadne announced, setting the leather-bound case on the bed. She frowned. "Why does your nightgown rattle?"

"Because those are my paint pots," Emily replied, sitting to accept her leather half boots from Daphne, who opened the travel case to shove in the slippers. "I stuffed my nightclothes in my reticule. Speaking of which . . ."

"I'll find it," Daphne said, going to search the wardrobe for the little drawstring handbag.

Ariadne sat next to Emily, her blue eyes thoughtful. "None of the others who joined the Royal Society for the Beaux Arts won the Barnsley Prize, you know. Lady St. Gregory invited them based on their work. I'm sure it will be the same for you."

"It will if I can persuade His Grace to dismiss these rumors of an engagement," Emily promised her. "I cannot *think* what Lord Robert is about. He couldn't be bothered to write over the last ten years since our parents spoke of us marrying, and yet he shows up today, bold as brass, and intends to carry me off without so much as a 'by your leave'!"

"Well, it was only an offer to escort you to London," Ariadne, ever the voice of reason, pointed out. "At least, that's what Miss Martingale told Mother."

Thank goodness she had, and thank *goodness* Ariadne had overheard and come straight to Emily as they were waiting in the Grand Salon after the graduation ceremony had ended. Otherwise, Emily would have been stuck in a carriage for the next two days with the arrogant fellow and would have no chance to beat him to her father to beg for a reprieve.

For what would she do if she found herself engaged so soon?

Some girls would count it a triumph, but to her it would be a disaster. She had plans for her Season, plans that did not include dancing attendance on the loathsome Lord Robert. Without the Prize in Art to recommend her, she must convince Lady St. Gregory to invite her into the Royal Society. Oh, that she might breathe that rarified air, rub shoulders with London's elite, see her paintings exhibited next to the best artists in all of England!

And worse, she might miss the ball! It would be just like him to insist upon it. Lord Robert had always been adept at getting his own way. As a child he had whined and sniffled and thrown tantrums for the least little refusal. If he had other plans, if he preferred his friends to hers, she would be stuck at his side with no chance to do any of the marvelous things she had planned.

"There, it's done," Priscilla announced, sailing into the room in a swirl of lavender lace. "Father has the carriage waiting. He was just as glad to escape before anyone could question him. Where did I put my traveling gown?"

"Here," Daphne offered helpfully, tossing the heavy gray wool at her. Priscilla caught it and tsked at the rough handling of the embroidered gown but quickly set about undoing the lace confection she wore. She had no trouble with the tapes, Emily noticed. Priscilla rarely had trouble with anything. All she had to do was bat those golden lashes, toss those golden curls, and the world fell at Priscilla's feet. It was equally unfair that she should have to run from graduation.

For Priscilla had her own reasons for fleeing the celebration going on downstairs. Like her father, she knew the dire consequences should their Dreaded Family Secret be revealed. She intended to give everyone something else to talk about by having the most elegant, exclusive ball that London had ever seen. The four girls had been planning it for months, going over every detail, dreaming of the moment they'd burst into Society and the world would be theirs.

Oh, why did Lord Robert Townsend have to spoil it!

"Hurry," Emily begged Priscilla, gathering up her things. Daphne had found Emily's reticule. The little bag was stretched out of proportion, bulging with her nightgown. She stuffed the crumpled lawn material down harder and yanked the cords of the bag tight.

"Stop fretting," Priscilla said, fastening the elaborate black braid that closed her gown. "Miss Martingale is far too busy cozying up to Acantha Dalrymple's father to bother about us. Besides, I had a vision last night for the ball." She lowered her voice and leaned toward them. "Goldfish."

Daphne, who had perched beside her sister on the bed, caught her breath as if Priscilla had imbued the word with mystic properties. Emily frowned. "Goldfish?"

"Indeed," Ariadne piped up, pulling her journal and pencil from her reticule as if to record the moment. "Remember the Celebration Dinner with the Allies last year? The prince had streams meandering down the table and real goldfish."

Trust Ariadne to remember. Her mind brimmed with everything she read: plays, pamphlets, poetry, prose.

Emily wrinkled her nose. "*The Times* reported the fish died halfway through dinner! I doubt the sight of rotting fish will do much to set the sophisticated tone you so desire, Pris."

Priscilla sniffed. "I'm quite certain my fish would not be so vulgar as to die before the final course." While Emily shook her head, Priscilla put on her straw bonnet. The glossy black feathers curled about one cheek. "There, all ready."

Emily had no reason to delay, yet she could not make herself leave. Priscilla tugged at the braided collar of her traveling gown as if she couldn't get it to sit properly. Daphne was swinging her full skirts against the side of the walnut bed as if she could not bear to set foot on the floor.

Adiadne cleared her throat. "I suppose you'd better go."

They all stared at one another.

Then Daphne leaped off the bed and enveloped Emily in a hug. "We'll send word the moment we reach London."

Priscilla and Ariadne joined them, arms tangling. Memories flowed from their touch: Ariadne hiding with Emily under the covers with smuggled lemon drops, Daphne trying to teach Priscilla to fence with the fireplace poker, Priscilla crossing her eyes at Emily as they waltzed with the vicar's ungainly twin sons. Once more Emily's eyes felt hot, but how silly! It wasn't the end; it was just the beginning!

Priscilla evidently thought the same, for she gave them all a squeeze. "Remember, we are La Petite Four, always together like matched cakes on a plate. The world will speak in reverent tones of the year Lady Emily Southwell, Priscilla Tate, and Daphne and Ariadne Courdebas made their debuts. You'll see."

"Where are you going?" a shrill voice demanded from the doorway.

Emily rolled her eyes, even as Daphne gave a muffled groan and Ariadne paled. Priscilla turned to face the vile creature who had tormented them all through school.

"Why, we're off to London, of course, Acantha," Priscilla said as if the girl were simple. "You'll want to return downstairs and accept congratulations. I'm certain your father at least is pleased you won back all the silly cups he paid for."

Acantha's thin lips tightened in her narrow face, and her long fingers smoothed over the engraved lettering on the cup she held. The Prize in Art! Emily fisted her hands to keep from ripping the thing from Acantha's grasp.

"Well," Acantha said, "I doubt I'd take so many of the cups if I hadn't some modicum of talent." She smiled as if she were genuinely sorry she was so talented and they were not.

Oh, how that smile lied.

"It does not signify," Emily said, taking Priscilla's arm and plowing forward so that Acantha was forced to pick up her spring green skirts and back out of the doorway. "We must go."

"Running away, are you?" Acantha sneered, following them. "A shame you don't dare face your beau without a cup in hand.

I'd be delighted to entertain him in your absence."

"Lord Robert Townsend is *not* my beau," Emily informed her.

"Though I'm certain Lady Emily will be only too happy to leave you with her castoffs," Priscilla said sweetly.

"At least I won't be *wearing* castoffs this Season," Acantha said, her free hand touching the perfect strand of Oriental pearls around her swanlike neck. They shone nearly as brightly as the hideous pomade she insisted on pouring over her lank brown hair.

Now Priscilla bristled. Oh, but Acantha was good at finding weaknesses! She poked and poked at you until she found the one place that hurt most.

Not today. Not anymore. "Pay her no heed," Emily told Priscilla. "Nothing she says will stop us."

"Oh, Miss Martingale!" Acantha sang out, high voice piercing the air. "Miss Martingale, Lady Emily is leaving!"

Very likely their headmistress could not hear Acantha, but Emily met Priscilla's gaze and saw the same fear written there. They could not be caught, or Emily was trapped. And the longer Priscilla remained at Barnsley, the more likely someone was to ask questions that were better off never answered.

As one, they turned and ran, past the startled Acantha, past Ariadne and Daphne, who waved in encouragement, right down the servants' stair to the ground floor.

Emily was once more breathless as they tumbled out into the kitchen. Everyone from the brawny footmen to the beefy cooks to the scrawny pot boy stopped and stared. Priscilla waved a regal hand. "I know we left you gifts this morning, but we simply wanted to share our best wishes and thank you again for your kind service these many years. Carry on."

They strolled out the door to the kitchen yard and promptly collapsed into giggles.

"I wish I could do that," Emily said. "I'd just sound rude."

Priscilla patted her feathered bonnet back into place. "I've learned it's all in how you present yourself. Now, let's find Father."

Good advice, but dozens of carriages lined the drive, some small and humble, others large and covered in gilt. One belonged to Lord Robert. Emily knew she could still be caught if she wasn't careful. She was so busy looking around that she nearly collided with a tall young man in a brown coat and trousers.

He reached out an arm to steady her. "Pardon me."

"My fault entirely," Emily assured him. She glanced up and stared. His hair was the color of a sunset on a stormy day, red and gold and brown blending in wild disarray, and his eyes were the gray of the storm. But his smile, well, his smile was positively wicked.

As if her stare amused him, he touched two fingers to his forehead. An odd salute. Who was he? She hadn't noticed him at the graduation ceremony. He couldn't be anyone's brother or cousin; she'd have heard.

"Emily!" Priscilla called ahead of her. "This way."

"Lady Emily!" Miss Martingale called behind her. "I must have a word with you."

She was caught! Her heart leaped into her throat, and she

clutched her locket with the absurd thought that it was the only thing holding her heart in her body. As the young man eyed her locket with a frown, she knew there was nothing for it. She lifted her dark green skirts, right in front of him, and ran once more.

+❖+ 2 +❖+

Thief!

"Finches," Priscilla said as the carriage rolled through the greening countryside on the way to London the next day. "We could set them amidst the roses I've ordered and have them serenade the guests. The ball is supposed to be an enchanted garden, after all. What do you think?"

Emily was too busy looking back to answer. Was that the dust of another carriage approaching, or merely the dust they'd left behind? Was that squeal from the Tate carriage's poorly made springs, or a voice ordering them to stop?

"Emily?" Priscilla said, a little louder.

Emily turned with a grimace. "Sorry. No finches, Pris. They'd fly into someone's hair, or worse."

"Oh, I suppose," Priscilla allowed. "But perhaps stuffed finches, then. Surely someone in London makes them. After all, we want this to be the most talked about event of the Season."

Mr. Tate, sitting across from them, managed a wan smile before turning his attention to the passing fields and hedges. Poor fellow. He couldn't afford what Priscilla needed to secure her an advantageous marriage, but if Priscilla didn't marry a wealthy gentleman, her father would have no money at all. Emily was glad His Grace had not put her in that position.

Of course, if he insisted on her marrying Lord Robert, that would be something else entirely. She reached for her locket, stroking the gold with her fingers.

And looked back once more. What if Lord Robert came pounding up on a black stallion and demanded her surrender? She couldn't relax until she'd spoken to His Grace and knew her plans were safe. And she couldn't quite attend to the plans for the wondrous ball until she'd figured out some way to show her paintings to Lady St. Gregory.

Lady St. Gregory was the president of the Royal Society for the Beaux Arts, the one trusted by the queen to enlist new members. She sculpted in marble. Ariadne had read them an account of the lady's most recent work just a month ago.

"A triumph of movement and emotion," *The Times* had said.

Surely Lady St. Gregory would see the triumph in Emily's work, even if Miss Martingale couldn't.

Emily wasn't sure whether it was the heady tang of turpentine or the feathery touch of a brush that first seduced her to the arts, but she was generally happiest at an easel. She often remembered the look on her beloved art teacher's face when Miss Alexander had seen Emily's *The Battle of Hastings*. In it, William the Conqueror stood high on a hill, banner waving in the breeze, while strung out around him, as far as the eye could see, lay the bodies of fallen Saxons. It had taken Emily all term to paint. Miss Alexander had gazed at it, dark eyes wide, and said, "Oh, Lady Emily, this is very, very good."

If only Lady St. Gregory would agree!

"I'm so glad we're having the ball," Priscilla said beside her, "rather than that little dinner Daphne and Ariadne's mother has planned for them. I've already had two hundred acceptances of the three hundred invitations that were sent, and we still have nine days to go. Even your Lady St. Gregory accepted," she added, as if sensing Emily's distraction.

That was it! Emily stared at her. "Oh, Pris, now I've had a vision. If I exhibited a painting at the ball, Lady St. Gregory would have to recognize me!"

Priscilla's eyes widened in obvious horror. "No, no, no. You cannot turn the ball into an art exhibition."

"What else can I do?" Emily asked. "His Grace is too busy to help me. His aunt, who was supposed to be my chaperone, is up in Cumbria helping my sister and Cousin Charles prepare for their first baby, and who knows when the child will arrive. I'll be lucky if I can leave the house until His Grace finds a replacement. The ball could be my only chance to gain Lady St. Gregory's attention!"

Priscilla grit her teeth, then raised a finger. "All right, you may display one, exactly one, painting at the ball. Perhaps I can persuade the orchestra to suffer it behind them on the platform."

That would never do. Lady St. Gregory might not even notice it. "No, Pris, if we do this, it must be up front."

Priscilla pressed her lips together as if she were trying to keep from saying something vile. Emily couldn't blame her for being vexed. Priscilla had inordinately high hopes for this ball. Like Emily, she might get only one chance to impress.

"Oh, as you wish," Priscilla said with a sigh. "I'll put it up front and surround it with a rose trellis. That should give it pride of place. But no battle scenes!"

Emily frowned. What did Priscilla expect, watercolor bowls of fruit? Not likely. Emily used oils, bold strokes, dark colors; she brought to life important subjects like the tragic deaths of heroes and glorious, blood-drenched battles. Her scenes were so real, she fancied she felt the beat of the drummer calling the march, heard the roar of canons in the distance. When she painted, she quite forgot that any other world existed.

"I'll try for something in keeping with the theme," she said. After all, there had been a War of the Roses, hadn't there?

Priscilla looked skeptical, but Emily turned to look back again. That problem had been solved, but what if Lord Robert reached London before them? What if he spoke to His Grace, her father, before she did?

No, she shouldn't worry. Ariadne had said Lord Robert's mother was with him, so he wouldn't rush. He'd told Miss Martingale they'd been visiting in the area and heard Emily required escort. What humbug. With His Grace just returned, she'd planned to ride home with Priscilla all along; her things had been packed and waiting for the Tate carriage.

Which simply did not travel fast enough.

Emily could not remain in her seat by the time they rolled into

London the next evening, joining Priscilla in pressing her nose against the glass of the carriage window to stare at the Great City. Massive stone buildings soared into the air, blocking the darkening sky. One set was gracefully classical, another heavy and pompous, a third sprawling in all directions surrounded by ornate columns. In the crowded cobblestone squares, hawkers called for violets, penny-a-sheet newspapers, roasted nuts. Everywhere was noise, movement, color. Emily's fingers trembled, and she wished she had her sketch book.

The Emerson family town house in the Mayfair district was just as impressive, at three stories tall. She'd never been there, but she approved of the elegant sweep of stone, the bright gleam of brass on the red-lacquered door. Mr. Tate assisted her down as footmen in dark coats and breeches hurried out to bring in her trunks and boxes.

Emily couldn't help the warmth that flooded her when she saw Warburton waiting for her. The butler had been with His Grace as long as she could remember, and his hair had been white nearly that long. When she was younger, she used to think that one day she'd grow tall enough to look him straight in his bright blue eyes. She'd long since resigned herself to the fact that that was never going to happen. No one was quite as tall as Warburton.

"Welcome home, your ladyship," he intoned, his usual calm self in the face of the bustle around him. The footmen hurried past to fetch in the rest of her belongings. "His Grace was delayed in Whitehall, but he hopes to join you for dinner."

She almost crumpled at his feet in relief. Dinner with her father was just the opening she needed to discuss this business of Lord Robert. Surely His Grace could be made to see reason. She would never want to disappoint him, but he knew how much she longed to join the Royal Society.

"Just see that you do not let Lord Robert Townsend near him," she told Warburton and went upstairs to change.

It was easy to guess which bedchamber was hers down the thickly carpeted hall. She merely had to follow the footmen carrying her things. As she paused in the doorway, she found herself rather pleased. The room was done in a Oriental theme, the walls adorned in painted silk showing white and black birds with tall crowns and long tails. The mahogany woodwork was trimmed in gold, and gold highlighted the tall window, dressing room door, and the spindles and headboard of the four-poster bed. Another time she might have been tempted to stretch out, but not when His Grace would be home so soon.

She had to keep busy or she would go mad!

She was instructing one of the footmen on how to set up her easel in an unused bedchamber across the corridor when she finally heard the front door. She left the fellow to hurry downstairs. With His Grace months at the Congress of Vienna, all Emily'd had were letters. She wanted to spend time with her father, hear his stories, tell him hers. Surely a few moments of his company, on her first night in London, was not too much to ask.

But the wood-paneled study on the second floor was empty in

the golden glow of candlelight, as was the stately dining room. The blue-and-gilt chairs of the withdrawing room waited expectantly. The other footmen had apparently retired to the kitchen to prepare for dinner, so she could not ask them where His Grace had gone. With a sigh, she went to check the sitting room, just in case her father might be entertaining a caller.

It was the most formal room she'd seen. Heavy red, brocaded drapes with gold-tasseled pulls covered the bow window, and red velvet chairs with clawed feet squatted before the fire's glow. She sucked in a breath when she sighted a gentleman standing next to them, then puffed it out as he turned and she recognized him.

The young man from Barnsley stood there, his hair glowing like flames in the light of the fire. How could he have beaten her to London? And if he had, did that mean Lord Robert was here as well? "How did you get here?" she demanded.

He offered her his wicked smile. "And good evening to you as well, Lady Emily," he said as he bowed.

Of course he knew her name. He'd obviously followed her. "Answer the question. How did you get here so quickly?"

He shrugged. "The mail coach moves quickly enough. And surely I'm not the first to seek an audience with His Grace."

Not the first, but one of the first she'd seen kept waiting by himself. "Who let you in?" she asked suspiciously.

"A busy footman. I thought it best to keep out of the way."

Emily gasped. "You sneaked in! Thief!" Small wonder his look had gone to her locket at Barnsley. Small wonder she hadn't recognized him when they'd first met. She did not make a habit of associating with thieves.

"Oh, there are thieves in London, all right," he agreed. He waved a hand to encompass the room. "You'd better watch out or you'll lose one of these fine paintings."

What fine paintings? His Grace owned any number of wonderful pieces from ages past, as well as some truly horrid portraits of their ancestors. She wasn't sure which he had ordered brought to London to decorate the town house.

But as she looked around the room, she recognized each painting as hers. *The Battle of Salamanca* hung over the fire, *The Battle of Hastings* was against the far wall, and *The Battle of the Nile* was to her right. It had been one of her first, when she hadn't quite mastered perspective. The British and French ships were all jumbled. He could not be much of a thief if he thought it fine art.

"What do you know of art?" she challenged.

He glanced out the open door. Then, as if satisfied that no one would approach them, he looked up to *The Battle of Salamanca*. She'd chosen a scene well-described in the papers. General Wellington had the French forces in the crossfire, with heavy casualties on both sides. His charger rearing, he held his saber aloft to order a charge. She'd never met the great man, but she fancied he'd be rather pleased with the piece.

"I don't know all that much about art," the young man before her admitted. "But I'd say this fellow never experienced war."

Emily stiffened. "Why? What did I . . . he get wrong?"

"Oh, the details are fine enough," he said. "I've known a few lads who served under Wellington on the Peninsula. This picture matches their tales, but it doesn't show their heart."

She frowned, moving closer. "What do you mean?"

He pointed to a fallen soldier. "Look here at this lad. He's gone down. Very likely he'll never see home or family again. He knows that by morning, crows will be picking at him. That's enough to give a man cause for thought, cause for fear. Does he look as if he's thinking about meeting his Maker?"

She had to own that he did not. While he was painted in exquisite detail, his perfect face showed no emotion whatsoever.

And was that so very bad? Not everyone had to cry!

"The purpose of the painting is not to show the individual soldier's feelings," she said, fingers tightening on her locket. "The purpose of the painting is to depict history."

He shrugged again. "There are books enough for that. Why bother painting it?"

"Why bother?" Emily sputtered, hand falling. "Sir, you have no sensibilities!"

Instead of taking offense, he merely laughed. Then he paused and nodded toward the door. "I've picked a poor time to visit, I see. You'll want to speak to your father. He's just come in."

"He has?" Emily hurried to the door and glanced out. His Grace had indeed entered the front door and was handing his top hat and walking stick to Warburton. He saw her peering out and smiled as he approached.

He was the perfect duke in her mind—not too tall, with sandy hair and knowing brown eyes. Every movement in his fine blue coat said confidence and privilege and power. Oh, but the gentleman in the sitting room was in trouble now. Emily turned with great pleasure to tell him so, only to find that he was gone, like smoke up a chimney, leaving the connecting door to the library ajar. Even as she stared in surprise, her father reached her.

"What a delightful homecoming," he said. "Not even presented to society and already engaged to be married."

Emily turned her stare on him, feeling as if the corridor had dipped beneath her feet. "What?"

He smiled fondly. "Lord Robert was so eager to tell me, he came to find me in Whitehall this afternoon. It seems he plans to marry immediately in Devonshire and sweep you off for a honeymoon. I am persuaded that he has grown into a fine young fellow. Congratulations, my dear. He's exactly the sort of man your mother and I always dreamed you'd marry."

3

A Handsome Devil

"No, no, no!" Priscilla cried the moment she heard the news. "You cannot run away to Devonshire. I cannot have the ball without you!"

La Petite Four had assembled in the Southwell withdrawing room late the next morning, their gowns draped softly across the blue upholstery of the chairs. Warburton had brought in sweets and tea for their enjoyment, but no one seemed particularly interested in enjoying themselves.

"We must have the ball," Ariadne was insisting, curls trembling on either side of her round face. "I've been practicing my witty conversation for weeks."

"What could His Grace be thinking?" Daphne lamented. "It just isn't done!" She pushed away the silver teapot as if she couldn't stand the thought of drinking at such a moment.

"I quite agree," Emily assured her. The idea still stunned her. Marriage? She'd only just graduated!

"I fail to see," Priscilla said, green eyes narrowing dangerously, "how Lord Robert can pull together a wedding in eight days, unless you plan to elope to Scotland."

Emily shuddered. "No, thank you. But then, I didn't plan to get married either. How would I even find time to be fitted for a wedding gown?"

"Surely Lord Robert gave you some sign of his affections," Ariadne said, reaching for a comfit Warburton had set out. "A lock of hair, a passionate letter." She popped the chewy confection into her mouth as if she feared the sugar would dirty her soft pink gown.

"Not a word," Emily said. "Though apparently His Grace had some inkling. He and Lord Robert's brother, the new Lord Wakenoak, have been discussing marriage settlements for months. They simply weren't sure Lord Robert wanted to settle down."

Of course, they hadn't asked her whether she wanted to settle down. Young ladies were supposed to desire marriage above all things. But this? Emily'd been so shocked by her father's announcement that she'd even forgotten to ask Warburton about the mysterious gentleman in the library until this morning.

"A Mr. James Cropper," her butler had said when she'd cornered him after breakfast. "He had a letter of introduction from a fine gentleman known to His Grace and wished to have words on a private matter, so it seemed appropriate to allow him to wait in the sitting room."

How very odd. Did thieves have letters of introduction?

"If he should call again," Emily had said, "I want you to find me straightaway." She supposed Mr. Cropper had not come calling today, for she'd heard nothing more.

Now Priscilla rose to pace the room. Her hair was as bright as the gilt chairs, and her blue muslin day dress with its white lace collar looked like a pale copy of the Wedgwood blue wallpaper.

"Then all is not lost," she declared. "We have only to convince Lord Robert that you must wait until after the ball. Think, Emily. What can we use against him?"

Emily raised her brows. "Against him? What do you plan, Pris, blackmail?"

Priscilla paused in her pacing. "If necessary."

"Surely we can reason with him," the ever logical Ariadne protested.

Emily could not feel so confident. Ever since her father had told her he agreed with Lord Robert's plans last night, she'd felt squished, her bones pressed together, as if her body were trying to curl into a snail's shell. She'd tried to protest, but her father had seemed so very happy about the entire matter that she couldn't find it in herself to disappoint him. Having her friends here now made it easier to breathe, and to think.

"Perhaps this isn't so horrid," Priscilla said, coming to sit near Emily on one of the delicate little blue chairs. "Some people might even say you're fortunate. With his family connections, Lord Robert is quite a catch."

Possibly, but Emily wished she understood *why* she'd caught him. It wasn't as if their lands marched side by side. His Grace's estates were all entailed to Cousin Charles, and she brought only a small estate from her mother to the marriage. And if it were a duke's consequence he craved, there must be other dukes with marriageable daughters. Why her?

"I still cannot like it," Daphne said, shifting in her gilt chair across from Emily. The weak spring sun, trickling through the windows, made the green sprigs on her white muslin dress look like little tufts of grass. "Lord Snedley is most particular about the way engagements are to be announced, and sneaking behind people's backs would not meet with his approval."

"Well, it isn't as if it were totally unexpected," Emily hedged, crossing her ankles under her heavy skirts. The spruce-colored wool gown had completely suited her mood that morning. "His father and mine talked of uniting our families forever. They were great friends in school. But I cannot believe that's all that motivates Lord Robert. When we were younger the only use he had for me was to torment me. He once snatched my riding crop and ordered me to kiss his boots before he'd give it back."

"You didn't!" Daphne gasped.

"No," Emily admitted. "I stomped on his instep. I was only thankful Mother noticed and put a stop to his wretched game. I only wish I knew what game he's playing now."

"It may not be a game," Priscilla said, leaning closer. "Your father said Lord Robert wishes this marriage. So long as Lord Robert allows the ball, I'd go along with him. The engagement will put you in the best position. You can flirt, and no one can get peeved because they'll all know you're taken."

"And you can eat whatever you like," Ariadne added, "without fear that you won't fit in your presentation gown." She reached for another comfit, and Daphne nudged her hand away.

"You see?" Priscilla said. "Besides, everyone will want to

congratulate you. As your dear friends, we'll be quite popular."

That was the one problem with Priscilla. She tended to think of her own needs first.

"But Priscilla," Daphne protested, "how could we enjoy ourselves, knowing we'd consigned Lady Emily to a monster?"

"Having a beastly childhood does not make Lord Robert a monster," Priscilla began when there was a cough at the door. Warburton met their gazes with a smile.

"Forgive the interruption, ladies, but the monster, that is Lord Robert, has come calling, and I wasn't sure you wished to receive him." He eyed the girls pointedly.

Emily raised her chin. "I'd very much like to have a word with him, Warburton. Please show him up."

"But do give us a few moments first, Mr. Warburton," Priscilla said sweetly.

Emily thanked him and turned to ask Priscilla why they needed time. But one look at her friends and she knew.

They were all primping.

She supposed she should do the same—fluffing up the curls on either side of her face, as Priscilla was doing or biting her lips to make them appear rosier, like Ariadne. She wasn't sure why Daphne was flapping her arms up and down like a goose, but she guessed it was on the fool-proof advice of Lord Snedley.

Still, Emily saw no need to posture for Lord Robert. He'd offered for her after ten years before he'd even seen her again! She was ready to level him immediately, tell him that under no circumstances would she marry him. But when he paused in the doorway a few moments later, words failed her.

He looked like one of the heroes in her paintings, tall and broad-shouldered. Against all odds, he had the same glorious mane of hair as Mr. Cropper, though it was artfully styled around his handsome face. His eyes were a deep clear blue that warmed with his smile. His dove gray coat and black trousers were so fitted, they showed nary a crease as he bowed.

Priscilla eyed him, Ariadne paled, and Daphne stared open-mouthed, despite all of Lord Snedley's sophisticated advice.

"Heaven is missing a few angels today, I see," he said as he straightened.

"I have read that line a dozen times before," Ariadne whispered to Emily. "He could do better."

Lord Robert evidently thought he'd done well, for his smile was confident as he strolled into the room. He went to Priscilla first, taking her hand and bringing it to his lips.

She smiled. "Such a pleasure to meet you, my lord. Lady Emily has told us so much about you."

And not a whit of it good. What was Pris thinking, smiling so fetchingly that dimples danced at the corners of her mouth? Lord Robert blinked as if he'd forgotten his own name, until some other emotion flashed across his face. Disappointment? Of course! He didn't know which one of the girls was Emily.

Emily rose. "You can stop the pleasantries. I'm not going to marry you."

He raised his brows, as if he had not expected her to attack and now must marshal his thoughts. Priscilla rolled her eyes as if begging heaven for help. Daphne nodded her support so vigorously, she was in danger of hitting her sister with her swinging curls.

"But of course you are, dear Lady Emily," he said, moving to her side. She caught the scent of cloves and had to stop herself from inhaling like a child in a kitchen with freshly baked cookies. He took her hand and kissed her knuckles. The warm pressure sent a shiver up her arm.

"I am your most devoted servant, I assure you," he murmured, releasing her. "I was crushed we could not meet at Barnsley, so I came here straightaway this morning."

As it was now nearly noon, she doubted he'd been in any particular hurry. Still, if he could be polite, then so could she. "These are my dear friends Priscilla Tate and Daphne and Ariadne Courdebas." Very likely she'd said their names so quickly, he wasn't at all sure who was who, but Lord Robert obligingly nodded to them all as Emily returned to her seat.

"Did I interrupt your conversation?" he asked politely, spreading his coattails to sit beside her.

Priscilla and Ariadne exchanged glances, and Emily glared at them in warning.

"We were discussing etiquette, my lord," Daphne announced, affixing him with a narrow-eyed look. "And how do you feel about the subject?"

Lord Robert pursed his lips. "I suppose I've never given it much thought. A gentleman is merely a gentleman."

Daphne frowned, but Priscilla jumped in. "And surely it is good etiquette to congratulate you, my lord. We were so excited to hear of your engagement."

Excited was hardly the word, but he could not know that as he smiled at Priscilla. "I am the most fortunate of mortals." He spread his arms along the top of the camel-backed sofa, and his fingers brushed Emily's shoulder. She should blush, giggle, bat his hand away, but she merely wanted to get up and walk out. She knew she was, by her nature, entirely too suspicious, but she could not shake the feeling that something was wrong. How could he be such a paragon? She'd always considered him a toad!

Priscilla clapped her hands together. "Oh, I just had a vision! We will toast your engagement at the ball! I've heard of the most cunning fountain, all bubbles and froth, and the ladies might dip their goblets for a taste. It will be the talk of London!"

Lord Robert withdrew his arm from Emily's shoulder, leaving her suddenly cold. "Ball? What ball?"

"My coming out ball," Priscilla said, dimples popping into view once more. "On April twelfth. Do say you'll come."

His smile was sad. "I regret that I cannot. Lady Emily and I will be in Devonshire by then, preparing to wed."

"We most certainly will *not*," Emily argued.

As he frowned, Priscilla put in smoothly, "Surely Lord Robert is teasing us. No gentleman would deprive his betrothed of her first Season." Emily thought she was not the only one who heard the steel behind the tone.

"It is with great regret that I must do so, Miss Tate," he assured her. "I'm sure Lady Emily mentioned to you that my dear father went to his reward this past October. My poor mother, Lady Wakenoak, is heartbroken. As this marriage was my father's dream, I ease her pain by honoring his wishes, particularly by marrying at our country seat in Devonshire."

"My condolences on your loss," Emily said, remembering His Grace mentioning Lord Wakenoak's passing in a letter and feeling like a selfish oaf for wanting to distress the poor widow further. "But I truly do not wish to wed, especially in the next eight days."

His russet brows drew together as if he were not certain what she was about.

Daphne nodded her support, curls bobbing. "We've been looking forward to this ball for ages, my lord. It is the pinnacle of our achievements and will signal to the world that we are ready to take our rightful places in Good Society."

"Well said," Ariadne put in admiringly. "I shall ask you to repeat that later so I can copy it into my journal."

As Daphne beamed, Lord Robert leaned closer to Emily. "Surely," he murmured, "we shouldn't quarrel over such a small matter, my pet."

Those lovely blue eyes pleaded for understanding. It was quite like looking into the coming night and the secrets it promised.

The thought set her cheeks aflame. Would all young men make her blush so? She'd have to rethink her wardrobe, or she'd spend the entire Season clashing with her skin!

"This is no small matter, sir," Priscilla said with a pointed look to Emily. "This ball is Lady Emily's chance to gain entrance to the Royal Society for the Beaux Arts."

The Royal Society. Her paintings. Her dreams made Lord Robert's lovely eyes fade in comparison. Emily rose once more, head high. Even the swish of her skirts sounded defiant. "Yes, Lord Robert. This ball may be my best opportunity to impress Lady St. Gregory. Joining the society is by her invitation, you know. It is the only way for me to become an acknowledged artist. Painting is my life's passion."

Propriety demanded that he rise as well, yet he gazed up at her, smiling still. "Now, now. I fear you will be too busy to paint. And we will be in Devonshire by this time next week, so you will not be able to attend Miss Tate's ball."

As Emily joined Priscilla in glaring at him, he rose at last. "Ladies, I should get to my purpose in calling. My mother is hosting a dinner party this Sunday to celebrate the engagement. Because His Grace is so busy, we'll likely sign the marriage settlements then as well. In any event, we'll make our bows to Society as the bride and groom to be. I trust you can all come."

Emily wanted to pick up the pot of tea and douse his ridiculous smile. He had the audacity to ruin her entire Season—nay, her entire life!—and then expected her and her friends to dine with him?

Had he no sensibilities? No refinement of spirit?

No idea he had laid down a challenge she had no choice but to accept? For she would not give up the ball or her painting, and Lord Robert Townsend would rue the day he dared to stop her.

❖ 4 ❖

*He Must Be
Up to Something*

She threw him out, of course. Or rather, she stalked out of the elegant withdrawing room, forcing him to follow, and led him down the carpeted stairs to Warburton.

"Our guest has a pressing engagement," she said. "Please see him out."

Lord Robert blinked, but his good manners apparently prevented him from arguing with her. He suffered himself to pick up his top hat and gloves and be ushered out the door by a dignified Warburton.

When Emily returned to the sitting room, she could see that her friends were not nearly so composed. Indeed, they looked as depressed as she felt. Priscilla was staring off in the distance, her chest rising and falling as if she was concentrating on taking deep, even breaths. Ariadne sat slumped in her chair, her reticule pooled in the lap of her gown like a wilted flower. Daphne chewed her lower lip and blinked rapidly, as if fighting tears. Either that or Lord Snedley advised blinking when faced with disaster.

Seeing Emily in the doorway, Priscilla rose to her feet and shook out her muslin skirts. "Everyone up. We have no time for this nonsense. We have much to do in the next eight days."

As Emily frowned, Daphne obligingly leaped to her feet, setting the teapot on the table beside her to clattering.

Ariadne got up more slowly. "What must we do?"

Priscilla waved her hands as if shooing away any potential objections. "Prepare for the ball, of course!"

Daphne brightened. "Then the ball is still on?"

"The ball," Priscilla said with a sniff, "was never off."

"Well said," Emily agreed, moving into the room. "But what do you know that I have missed, Pris?"

Priscilla raised her chin so that her golden curls caught the sunlight. "Only that you cannot listen to Lord Robert. Some gentlemen are entirely too full of themselves, and I can see that he's one of them."

"I told you he was not to be trusted," Daphne added. "'A gentleman is merely a gentleman' indeed." She rolled her sky blue eyes. "Perhaps *he* should read Lord Snedley."

Emily knew she should probably invite them to sit back down and have a cup of tea, but the silver pot and the dainty flowered china cups had never looked less inviting. Instead she wandered to the window and gazed out at the garden below. Tulips lined the redbrick path to the stables, and wrens darted about, as if they enjoyed their freedom. Was she never to have any?

"Lord Robert has always been arrogant," Emily told her friends. "Though he's only a second son, he puts on the airs of a prince. At least he is thinking of his family instead of himself for once." She puffed out a sigh that fogged the glass. "Still, I cannot quite believe he is reformed. Why agree to marry me? Why must we wed now, when the season has barely started? Why must we rusticate in Devonshire?" She turned to face the others. "He must be up to something."

Priscilla sighed as well. "I never have understood why you must see the dark in every situation, Emily, but I fear you're right this time."

Ariadne rubbed a hand over the gilded wood of her chair. "Perhaps his love of Emily motivates him. Perhaps he cannot bear to share her with the rest of the world." She brightened. "Oh, that's good."

Priscilla shook her head. "If he truly loved her, he would want her to be happy. How can she possibly be happy if we must cancel the ball?"

"He didn't say you must cancel it," Ariadne reminded her. "Only that Lady Emily cannot attend. You could still come out."

Priscilla touched her slender neck as if she felt unseen hands strangling her. "Impossible. Even if Lady Emily did not wish to impress Lady St. Gregory, she must attend. Mother's told everyone the Duke of Emerson's daughter is a dear friend. The prince won't come just to see me, and neither will a great many others in London Society, not after Aunt Sylvia's fall from grace. We may have hidden the full extent of the scandal, but they'll all have heard she's now residing with keepers." She uttered that last word so quietly it was almost inaudible.

Ariadne's and Daphne's faces melted into pity. Emily knew hers must look much the same.

"It isn't your fault your aunt went mad and tried to smother Lord Brentfield with a feather pillow," Ariadne assured Priscilla. "Who could possibly have foreseen that outcome?"

They all nodded. They had discussed last month's strange events at Brentfield Manor so many times that there was no need to go over the fine points. Priscilla's aunt Sylvia had grown greedy, pure and simple. Unsatisfied with the money she received as a widow, she'd set her cap at the new Lord Brentfield instead. When the fellow had preferred their art-teacher-turned-chaperone to her, Sylvia tried to kill him. She might have succeeded if Emily hadn't suspected her. And if Priscilla's aunt hadn't taken a bad fall trying to escape, the woman might even now be in Newgate Prison, waiting to be hanged.

And wouldn't that have been a terrible scandal!

"Aunt Sylvia's madness surprised everyone," Priscilla said now, lowering her gaze and tracing a pattern in the carpet with the toe of her blue leather slipper, "most of all my parents. Besides, it was Aunt Sylvia's money that paid for my gowns, the Elysium Assembly Rooms for the ball, the one thousand crimson roses. There's nothing left. If I am to redeem us, I must marry well."

"But what of love?" Ariadne asked with a frown.

Priscilla raised her head and tossed her curls. "I imagine love and compatibility are very nice for those who can afford them. After this business with Aunt Sylvia, I have no choice but to look for more."

Emily sighed. "And in doing so, you settle for less."

Priscilla's fingers tightened at her sides. "Do you think I like it? But every day I'm reminded of the necessity. Father is a shadow of himself, scuttling around as if he caused the scandal. Mother has lost all confidence. She frets and moans over every decision, as if my debut alone can save us."

Emily crossed the room to her side and lay a hand on her arm. "I am truly sorry for your aunt's madness. You do deserve better."

Tears clustered on Priscilla's golden lashes. "And you deserve a handsome, charming husband who appreciates your art. You also deserve the most wonderful ball any artist has ever received." She stomped her foot as if to set her mark on the matter. "Let me find Mr. Warburton, and I'll show you!"

⸎ 5 ⸎

To Squander One's
Dowry on Fripperies

Emily wasn't sure what Priscilla intended, but, in very short order, the four girls found themselves in His Grace's green-lacquered town carriage, rumbling past Hyde Park. Priscilla was ever good at managing. Between her charm and her own good sense, she could convince most anyone to do most anything.

A shame Lord Robert was not more susceptible.

"But where are we going?" Ariadne asked, peering out the window at the elegant town houses that lined Park Lane. Beside her, out the opposite window, Daphne was obviously watching the horses and riders making the most of the rare spring sunshine and exercising on Rotten Row, the sandy track that ran along the edge of the park.

"You'll see when we get there," Priscilla promised.

A few moments later, Mr. Phillips, His Grace's coachman, pulled the carriage up in front of a three-story building of white stone, with fluted columns along the front and a stonework ledge between the first and second floors.

Ariadne evidently recognized it from Priscilla's descriptions. "The Elysium Assembly Rooms! This is where we're going to have the ball!"

Emily felt a lurch that had nothing to do with the coach. It was more like the world had righted itself at last. This was where she would triumph. She could feel it.

"Indeed," Priscilla said as the groom opened the carriage door to help her out onto the stone pavement. "I thought it high time we all saw the place."

Emily could only agree, but Ariadne protested as they followed her out. "But someone would have to let us in."

Priscilla smiled and snapped open her white lace parasol as if to shield herself from any other concerns. "Of course. Which is why I asked Mr. Warburton to dispatch a footman before we ordered round the carriage."

A small gentleman in a long, dark coat and darker trousers was waiting for them inside. Before Emily could gain more than an impression of light wood and polished floors in the entryway, he'd thrown open the doors to the ballroom itself.

There it was, the room they'd been dreaming about. Emily stepped through the tall double doors, the sound of her slippers as soft as the tiptoe of a kitten. She could feel the others fanning out behind her, gazing around them.

"Oh, my," Daphne said, and her awed voice echoed.

Priscilla ventured into the cavern of a room, letting her free hand trail along the first of the dozen alabaster columns. Emily's gaze followed the fluted white column up the nearly two stories to the gilded, domed ceiling where hung two chandeliers, with tier upon tier of sparkling crystal that tinkled faintly in the breeze from the open door. She'd thought Priscilla's invitation list of three hundred people a bit ambitious, but nearly twice that many could have fit within the ballroom.

Priscilla closed her parasol and used it as a baton. "There," she said, pointing to the recesses running behind the columns on either side of the room. "That's where our family and friends shall sit to watch us dance or promenade. And there, on the right, is where we'll place buffet tables, covered with delicacies. And near the entrance I'll have the receiving line, to graciously greet each guest."

Daphne had wandered across the room to another set of double doors. "Here's the garden," she called. "And a lovely veranda, just right for taking a little air between dances."

Ariadne sighed. "Or exchanging a moonlight kiss."

Turning, Daphne tapped a foot against one of the polished stone tiles inlaid in the center floor, then lifted her skirts and slid a few feet. She grinned until she caught Emily's gaze, then stood straighter, marched up to her, and swept her a bow.

"May I have this dance?"

Emily couldn't help grinning as well. Before she knew it, Daphne had taken her hands and was twirling her about the floor. The air caressing her face smelled of beeswax and lemon, but she knew the night of the ball it would be scented with roses and the lavender and violet scents of ladies in fine silk. The music would dance on the air more lightly than the waltz Ariadne was humming from the musicians' platform, where she waved her hand as if conducting a ghost orchestra that sat among the golden stands and little gilt chairs.

And La Petite Four would all be dancing with fine gentlemen in black jackets and spotless white cravats. Priscilla swayed back and forth, gazing up as if she were already imagining what it would feel like to be held in the arms of a very handsome fellow who found her utterly charming. Of how it would feel to finally join Society, to be seen as a true lady at last.

Then something warm and strong rose up inside Emily like a hot-air balloon ascending over Hyde Park. She spun out of Daphne's hold, her skirts billowing, a laugh bubbling up. Daphne started laughing as well, and Ariadne and Priscilla quickly joined in. The joyous sound echoed to the ceiling, filling the room, filling her.

To think that just because of Lord Robert Townsend, she could lose all this!

Emily spun to a halt, sobering. "We must stop him."

The smile faded from Daphne's face. "We must."

Ariadne climbed down from the musicians' platform as Priscilla moved closer. "Agreed," Priscilla said. "It might help if you told your father how selfish Lord Robert is being."

Emily shook her head. "His Grace doesn't see it as selfishness. He thinks it perfectly fine that I forgo the ball, that I marry immediately. No, we must make him see that Lord Robert Townsend is not the man for me."

"How?" Ariadne asked, joining them as well.

Emily sighed. "If only I could prove he was up to something nefarious. I know he must be. Why refuse the ball? I cannot help but think there is more here than meets the eye."

"Like what?" Daphne asked, obviously fascinated.

"Who can say?" Emily said with a shrug. "Some kind of ulterior purpose. Perhaps he hopes to squander my dowry on fripperies."

Ariadne stuck out her lower lip. "If I were writing the scene, I'd say he'll use your father's consequence to engage in some criminal activity—like smuggling young ladies of good family to be sold in the slave markets of the far East."

Priscilla laughed. "Only you could come up with such a tale."

Ariadne smiled. "Why, thank you."

"I need more than a story," Emily told them. "His Grace is ever practical. I need facts, proof."

"With Lord Robert as your fiancé," Daphne put in, "you'll be expected to spend time together. That should give you an opportunity to learn his secrets."

Priscilla shook her head. "There isn't enough time before the ball. What if you hired a Bow Street Runner? You know, the fellows who investigate crimes?"

"And told them what?" Emily replied. "That I wish to investigate Lord Robert because he won't let me attend a ball? They'd laugh me out of the magistrate's office."

"Ask a servant to follow him, then," Daphne suggested.

"His Grace is already running short-staffed. Warburton will hire some help for the Season soon, but they'll be new and I couldn't be certain I could trust them."

"I think," Ariadne announced with great feeling, "that *we* should be the ones to mount an investigation, just like the gallant men of Bow Street." She stood taller, as if trying to make the most of her small stature. "I've read any number of stories in which the Bow Street Runners question family, acquaintances, servants. They've been known to follow a criminal all over England to catch him in the act. I daresay if we tried it, we'd have a better picture of Lord Robert." She glanced around, as if expecting censure.

Priscilla's smile widened. "Brilliant."

Daphne nodded. "I could not have devised a better plan myself."

Emily looked at her with surprise. "But surely Lord Snedley would find it improper in the extreme."

Daphne blinked. "Only if we are caught."

"Which I do not intend to be," Priscilla said gravely, one arm wrapped about the waist of her soft blue gown. "There's scandal enough already."

"You don't have to come, Pris," Emily said. "I have Father's consequence to hide behind, and Daphne and Ariadne have their mother's renowned sense of decorum. *You* have the most to lose."

Priscilla dropped her arm. "Precisely. Which is why I must go with you. La Petite Four must discover Lord Robert's secret and save the ball, and if that means following him from one gaming hell and pleasure palace to another then so be it!"

❖ 6 ❖

A Duchess Never Drives in Puce

They left the Elysium Assembly Rooms with great purpose. Ariadne drew her leather-bound journal from her reticule and proceeded to draft a plan that included interviewing Lord Robert's friends, family, and servants, as well as watching the man himself.

"I have read," she said as she wrote, "that a gentleman is generally found during the day at his club."

"But which club?" Priscilla replied. "My father once belonged to White's, Brooks's, and Boodle's, all at the same time!"

Neither did they know Lord Robert's intimates. Which of the fine gentlemen strolling and riding through the park, top hats dark in the sunlight, might be privy to his secrets? They could hardly accost the fellows and ask!

In the end, they decided to start at the Townsend town house. As Lady Emily could visit the Townsends as often as she liked, now being affianced to Lord Robert, she did not think His Grace would be concerned if she kept the carriage a bit longer. Goodness knows, she was delighted to have an excuse to get out of the house!

Priscilla seemed just as pleased. "When I am a duchess," she said, running her hand over the plump cushions, "I shall insist on velvet in all my coaches, a different color and coach for each day. I think Tuesday will be a fine blue, like this."

"What if you decide to drive in puce on a Tuesday?" Daphne asked.

Priscilla looked down her nose at her. "A duchess never drives in puce."

"I suppose," Emily said, "it depends on the duke. They are generally old and crotchety, Pris, except for His Grace."

"You are referring to the royal dukes, the brothers of the prince," Priscilla said with a sniff. "Of course I would not settle for one of those. I rather thought I'd seek introduction to the Duke of Rottenford. He's said to be rather dashing."

"He's the youngest of the bachelor dukes and has a fortune of ten thousand pounds per annum and a seat just outside London," Ariadne said. "I read it in *DeBrett's Peerage*."

"You see?" Priscilla said with a sigh. "He's perfect."

Emily felt nearly as breathless. She would never have thought it possible, but it was rather a lark to be dashing about after a gentleman, trying to discover his secrets. What would she learn about Lord Robert today? Daphne must have had the same thought, for she was fairly bouncing against the cushions, putting herself in danger of crushing her straw bonnet against the paneled ceiling.

"What do you think Lord Robert is doing right now?" she asked as the carriage trundled through Mayfair, passing town houses as grand and even grander than His Grace's.

"Going to a cunning loan broker to borrow gambling money against Lady Emily's dowry," Ariadne predicted. "Or to whoever helps him dispose of the virgins he's probably selling into slavery."

"Consulting with his tailor, more likely," Priscilla said. "We shall be lucky if we find him at home."

They were quite unlucky indeed. The carriage stopped before a tall, redbrick town house with green shutters on the multi-paned windows and a large park opposite in the center of the square. When Lady Emily showed the wizened butler the calling card His Grace had had made for her, he reported that neither Lady Wakenoak nor Lord Robert was at home.

"It is the Season," Priscilla reminded them as they returned to the carriage.

Emily frowned back at the dark green-lacquered door engraved with a lion's head. "True, but if Lady Wakenoak is so devastated by her husband's loss, why is she out making calls?"

"At the very least," Daphne agreed, "there should be a black wreath on the door to show they are in mourning. Lord Snedley advises at least a year for a husband, more for someone you loved."

Emily eyed her. "Then shouldn't Lord Robert also be in mourning for his father? If Lady Wakenoak is supposed to forgo Society, why may Lord Robert marry? What does the sainted Lord Snedley advise for a son?"

"To spend his inheritance as soon as possible," Daphne replied cheerfully.

Well, that was no help. As they settled in the carriage once more, Emily thought hard. London was so large. How could they possibly trace Lord Robert's footsteps? She gazed at the park in the center of the square. The trees were leafing out in a bright spring green, and the daffodils were just beginning to bloom, bending over the grass like yellow teacups. It wasn't hard to spot the young man, standing just inside the path that led through the center of the garden as if he had been waiting for her. She recognized that mop of russet hair that begged to be painted. Emily didn't dare move even within the carriage, lest he notice.

"Pris," she hissed, "do you see the man standing under the trees over there?"

Immediately Daphne and Ariadne craned their necks as well.

"The fellow with the common coat?" Priscilla asked.

"The mysterious stranger with the muscular build?" Ariadne added.

"The gentleman standing in the Terpsichorean Slouch that Lord Snedley favors?" Daphne put in.

"Yes!" Emily whispered. "His name is James Cropper. He was at Barnsley, and he tried to see His Grace last night."

Daphne gasped. "Is he following you?"

Emily shook her head. "I thought so at first, but I can see no reason for it. Still, he may know where Lord Robert has gone, and I intend to find out."

She reached for the door handle, but Ariadne caught her arm. "You can't go out there!"

Emily started to protest, but Priscilla was nodding, her lovely face solemn.

"She's quite right, Emily. You're betrothed and shouldn't be seen with another man." She turned to Daphne. "You go."

Daphne stared at them all, her blue eyes narrowed. "Why do you always ask me to do such things? Priscilla never dashes through the bushes; she knows better than to ruin her gown. And Ariadne never peeks around corners or hides behind horses."

Ariadne shrugged. "I know what happens at that end of the beast."

"So do I," Daphne declared, nose in the air. "And I am *trying* to be a lady. What gentleman wants to marry a girl with more dash and skill than he has?"

Emily couldn't wait for them to decide. "There, he's ducked deeper into the shadows. We'll lose him!" She turned the brass handle, clambered from the coach, and waved to Mr. Phillips to wait.

Daphne climbed down behind her. "Oh, very well," Emily heard her mutter as Daphne caught up. "I'll come along, but only to give you a proper chaperone."

They hurried across the street. Emily peered around the bushes at the edge of the park and over the top of shrubs. Where had he gone? What was she to do, drag Daphne through the undergrowth in search of him?

Daphne apparently had other ideas. She linked her arm in Emily's.

"Lovely day for a walk, isn't it?" she said in an unusually loud voice, pulling Emily along the pebbled path lined with daffodils that led deeper into the park. "I'm so glad you insisted upon it."

What on earth was wrong with her? Had she gone as mad as

Priscilla's aunt? As if Daphne knew Emily's thoughts by the frown, she offered her a broad wink and waited expectantly.

Oh, of course! She was using subterfuge. Rather wise, actually. Whether Daphne liked it or not, there truly was a reason they asked her to do things like this.

"Ah, yes," Emily said, though she could not manage quite so bright a tone. "A lovely day. Shall we stroll?"

"I'd be delighted." Daphne continued at a leisurely pace across the park. Her eyes were narrowed, gaze darting about, as if she could see through the greening shrubbery. Daphne's sky blue gaze had held the same look when she and Emily had joined His Grace for a fox hunt. She had watched, carefully, from horseback as the hounds coursed across the fields, like streams rushing in the spring. It was easy to spot the moment when they all coalesced, caught the scent, and took off in pursuit.

"He's just gone to ground," Daphne whispered to Emily. "But we shall catch him."

Emily kept the smile on her face. "Do you see him?" she whispered back.

"Not at the moment . . . wait! To your right, behind that laurel shrub."

Something was indeed moving there, and Emily fancied she caught a glimpse of russet hair. Excitement coursed through her, sharp and bold, and she could feel Daphne's grip tighten on her arm. Their footsteps quickened.

"You could not ask for a finer day," Emily said as they closed in on him. She hoped Daphne was the only one who heard the tension in the tone.

"Unseasonably warm," Daphne agreed, keeping an eye on their quarry. He seemed to have crouched down, as if to spy on them. The bushes rustled with his movement.

Emily froze, heart pounding. What would he do, knowing he'd been caught? What would he say? Her fingers went to the curls at the side of her straw bonnet as if they needed some anchor.

Or wanted her to primp.

"Say something," Daphne hissed. "You're so brave. Confront him."

Emily knew she should. She was the daughter of the duke, after all. She should stand tall, demand that he come out, order the thief to explain himself. She'd had no trouble telling Lord Robert how she felt in the withdrawing room that morning. Why couldn't she open her mouth now?

The bushes rustled again, more forcefully this time, and Emily took a step back. Her fingers clutched Daphne's arm so tightly, she thought she might break Daphne's bones. Daphne was just as frozen.

"I cannot recall Lord Snedley discussing the finer points of stalking a gentleman through the park," she whispered to Emily. "What shall we do?"

Something large and powerful shifted its weight, and Emily sucked in a breath. Eyes wide, Daphne removed Emily's fingers from her arm and dropped a curtsy.

"Forgive me, sir," she said to the bush. "Have we met?"

Emily stared at her.

Mr. Cropper was not nearly so civil. He growled! Emily took another step back in alarm, pulling Daphne with her. The bushes were shoved aside, and before Emily could cry out, a furry body launched itself at them. The creature hit Daphne in the chest, tearing her away from Emily as Daphne careened backward to land on her rump in the dirt of the path.

Emily rushed to her rescue, but it was too late. Daphne surrendered herself to a very wet kiss.

"Down!" she commanded, and the Airedale obediently climbed off her and lay down at her side. An elderly footman who had obviously been taking the dog for a walk hurried up, red-faced.

"I'm so sorry, miss. He slipped the leash. Are you all right?"

"Fine," Daphne said, accepting his hand to allow her to rise. "Dogs love me. A shame I can't say the same about the gentlemen."

Emily shook her head. Her hand was on her chest, and she felt her heart still pounding its wild beat. Glancing around, she saw no sign of the mysterious Mr. Cropper.

But that didn't mean she wouldn't catch him, or Lord Robert, the next time. It seemed they needed more cunning to catch the fox in the eight short days left to them.

The next step in their investigation, according to Ariadne, was to interview Lord Robert's servants. Emily didn't have much hope there, as she hadn't even been let into the Townsend town house. Besides, there was a question of loyalty.

No, it would be better to question someone well-versed in the ways of society, someone who had the ear of servants and aristocracy alike, someone she trusted.

In a word, Warburton.

❖ 7 ❖

Sinful Gossip

"Have you heard any rumors about the Townsends?" Emily asked her butler that evening as Warburton served her dinner on a silver tray in the quiet of her room. His Grace had been called to dine with the prime minister, and Emily abhorred sitting alone in the elegant dining room, eating at one end of the big empty damask-draped table.

Warburton seemed to sense her discomfort, for he went out of his way to place a tasseled pillow at her back where she sat on a black-and-white-striped satin chair near the cozy fire and to set a black satin footstool with gold fringe at her feet. His brows drew together as he straightened from placing a damask napkin across her lap.

"Rumors about the Townsends?" he responded at last, picking up the book she had been reading before he entered and gazing at the spine as if he was fascinated by the topic of a young lady's adventure in a cursed castle. "I'm sure I couldn't say, your ladyship."

She took the book from his hands and laid it aside, refusing to let him get away so easily. "Couldn't say or won't? If you will not tell me, Mr. Warburton, I will imagine the worst." Her silver fork flashed as she picked it up. "Does Lord Robert beat his servants?"

Warburton drew himself up. "Certainly not. You must remember—they serve his brother, and the present Lord Wakenoak would not countenance such behavior toward the staff, even though he has been a bit lax in paying them."

Emily selected a piece of choice lamb and chewed slowly. So Lord Robert's brother stiffed the staff. Reprehensible, but nothing she could lay at Robert's door. Unless their lack of funds had something to do with his behavior. She swallowed and cocked her head. "I fear Lord Robert gambles."

"Likely less than his father before him."

That was most unhelpful. She had no idea how much the former Lord Wakenoak had enjoyed the cards.

"Did his father gamble a great deal?"

"Perhaps more than is generally considered wise."

Interesting, she thought, using her fork to toy with her dilled carrots. Too bad Warburton's tidbit offered her nothing in her quest to discredit Lord Robert. She eyed her butler as he towered over her. "Does Lord Robert keep a mistress?"

Warburton met her gaze by looking down his impressive nose. "That is not a conversation His Grace would want me to have with you."

Her cheeks heated. He was quite right; it was a bold question. "But it is a conversation I must have," she protested, wiggling on the satin seat, "if I am to understand Lord Robert."

"Then I suspect it is a conversation you should have with Lord Robert."

He had a point. How would Robert react if she mentioned the matter? She pictured his stunned look and grinned.

Of course, he could be no more stunned than Mary was when Emily began the same conversation with her maid later that night before bed.

Mary was dark-haired and darker-eyed and a little on the pale side, or perhaps Emily just terrified her. Mr. Phillips had confided that Mary had been His Grace's upstairs maid in London until she agreed to take on extra duties while Emily was there. His Grace didn't apparently see the need to hire Emily her own maid even though she was out of school. She could only hope that was not because he thought she was going to marry soon, and then it would be up to Lord Robert to see to all her needs.

"Rumors?" Mary said, fair skin turning even paler.

Perhaps if she didn't look directly at the woman, Mary would be less nervous. Emily turned to let the maid unlace her quilted cotton corset. "Yes, rumors, stories. Gossip."

"Well," Mary said, busily pulling the cord through the holes in the back of the undergarment, "everyone seems quite glad Lord Robert has chosen to settle down."

"Settle down from what?" Emily asked with a frown.

Mary's fingers seemed to slow. "Oh, I'm sure I couldn't say, your ladyship."

Not her too. This would never do! "It's quite all right to speak freely, Mary," she said as gently as she could. "I won't scold, I promise."

Mary sighed as she finished with the corset and pulled it off, her breath brushing Emily's bare shoulder. "It's just that I want to do a good job for you, your ladyship. Being a lady's maid has always been my dream."

"I understand having a dream," Emily said, turning to face her once again. "Lord Robert is currently threatening mine. So, please, tell me if you know. Why did he have to settle down?"

Mary clutched the corset to her chest and lowered her voice, as if afraid the silk-covered walls might overhear. "He was a wild fellow, your ladyship. The other servants were talking about how he had a girl in every village around the family's country estate. Even dallied with a merchant's daughter here in town and a married lady."

Oh, the cad! Hadn't she said he was up to no good? Emily could feel herself blushing just thinking about it.

Mary must have noticed that Emily had reddened, for the maid hurried to fetch her robe.

"Now, don't you worry, your ladyship," she said, draping the quilted satin around Emily's shoulders. "He chose you, didn't he? That proves he intends to do right."

Perhaps. But it might also prove that he'd simply bowed to pressure from his family. What better way to turn respectable than to marry the daughter of an old family friend, particularly when she was the daughter of a duke? There was *nothing* more respectable than marrying the daughter of a duke. Yet why the hurry? Just how tame was Lord Robert Townsend now?

The thought kept Emily up late into the night. Unfortunately, Mary had handed her nothing she could use. Obviously His Grace knew all about Lord Robert's reformation. He'd said he and Robert's brother had only been waiting for Robert to change before announcing the wedding plans. So she still had nothing she could tell her father that would change his mind and save the ball.

And it wasn't as if she cared who Robert had dallied with. She certainly didn't want him to fall in love with her! But she'd thought, she'd *hoped*, that the man she married would see more in her than merely her father's consequence and good name. Was it not possible that someone might enjoy her company, appreciate her art, want to be with her simply for herself?

She finally rose, pulled on her painting smock, and went to her easel. She was itching to start another battle scene. She could just imagine all those feudal fighters in the colors of Lancaster and York. At least their roses weren't pink.

She despised pink.

Truly, was there ever a more insipid color? It neither made the bold statement of red nor whispered the purity of white. Yet she was convinced that His Grace would be the happiest of all men if she wore nothing but that color. Pink, he seemed to think, was singularly feminine.

It was simply not her.

Candlelight flickering around the room, she set up the larger of the two seasoned canvases that Miss Alexander had sent with her to London and stood staring at the creamy surface before sketching out the basic scene. It would be a huge clash, the battle lines wavering, bodies strewn from here to the far horizon, her most glorious work yet. And maybe, in the foreground, a single trampled rose. She set to work laying it all out.

But she could not seem to concentrate on her painting either. She kept looking at the soldiers on the battlefield and wondering how they felt. Were they frightened, fighting brothers, friends? Did they feel alone? Abandoned? Did they wish their mothers were close by, whispering encouragement, soothing fears?

She did.

Emily set down her tools and reached for her locket, opening it for a moment to gaze at the tiny portrait inside. If only she could paint something of worth, something that would make Lady St. Gregory welcome Emily into the Royal Society with open arms. What could be finer than the company of other artists, people who thought like she did, people who understood and respected her? She could not let Lord Robert spoil that future for her. She *would* not.

She took a deep breath and got back to work.

❖ 8 ❖

On Bond Street
Without a Chaperone

Late the next morning, Emily was trying to determine precisely how blood would pool around a decapitated body when the footman announced she had visitors. Priscilla, Daphne, and Ariadne were eager to hear what she'd learned from her servants, but Emily only agreed to tell them after they promised to pose for her battle scene.

She would have preferred to use the footmen. Unfortunately, the last time she'd asked, two had become so carried away that a Chinese vase had been damaged, and Warburton had asked her not to involve the staff again.

As it was, only Daphne could stand straight and valiant enough to do Emily any good as a model soldier (though she was pleased to discover that Ariadne made an excellent corpse). Priscilla insisted on playing a duchess watching from the edge of the battlefield. Emily pointed out that duchesses, or most dukes for that matter, seldom went to war, but Priscilla was adamant, so Emily let it go at that.

"So," she said as she studied the angle of Daphne's chin, "we know that Lord Robert Townsend has no money and likes the ladies all too well."

"Definitely not hero material," Ariadne said, raising her head into a patch of sunlight that turned her hair to gold.

Emily wanted to disagree, but she couldn't, so she merely ordered Ariadne to lie back down like a good corpse.

"It isn't enough," Priscilla said with a sigh. "A great many people find themselves with less money than they'd like. That doesn't make them criminals."

"But how is Lady Emily to know?" Ariadne asked from the floor.

"An excellent question," Emily replied. "Please forgive me, Ariadne, but I deviated from your plan. First thing this morning, I sent one of our footmen with a note asking if Lord Robert would come calling this afternoon. I thought perhaps I'd get him to take me to see the Parthenon Marbles."

Ariadne smiled. "An excellent strategy. Draw him out."

Emily sighed as she stroked her brush across the oil on her palette. "I thought so. Unfortunately, he already answered me. He is too busy today to assist me but will take me to see the Marbles tomorrow. The footman reported that Lord Robert must shop this morning, and this afternoon he will be preparing to attend the Marchioness of Skelcroft's ball."

"Well, I like that," Priscilla scoffed, eyes narrowing. "He's only too happy to attend a ball when it isn't ours!"

"That seems most unfair," Daphne agreed.

"He must have some reason," Ariadne insisted. "Could the marchioness be the married lady with whom he'd dallied?"

Emily's hand jerked, smearing her stroke. She set the brush

and palette down before she could do more damage. "I suppose I shall have to ask him."

Ariadne's eyes widened, and even Priscilla looked impressed, hurrying out of her pose at the edge of the thick carpet.

Daphne shook her head. "But you can't. You don't even have a chaperone."

"Yes, whatever happened to your aunt Minerva?" Priscilla asked, moving to Emily's side and frowning at the painting.

"Warburton insists that she is expected any day, but I have my doubts. Why would she come to London with the prospect of a new baby to cuddle? No, I simply cannot wait for her company to ask Lord Robert. I cannot wait even until tomorrow. We only have *seven days*. I must act now."

"Well," Priscilla said, "we can't get ourselves invited to the marchioness's ball tonight, but if Lord Robert is currently out shopping, you can be certain where he'll be at some point or other."

Ariadne and Daphne nodded. "Bond Street," they chorused.

And that was how they all arrived on Bond Street, in search of Lord Robert.

Warburton hadn't protested when Emily mentioned that the four of them would be together in the most famous shopping district in London on this sunny day. He'd even volunteered the carriage again. Emily's nose was once more to the glass of the carriage's windowpane as Mr. Phillips maneuvered the horses down Brooke Street and out into the bustling crowds along New Bond Street.

Fashionable shops hugged the street, their front windows displaying all manner of wonders, from satins that caught the light in a rainbow of colors to cakes topped with sugared plums. Everywhere strolled ladies in feathered hats, gentleman in shining boots. Maids with parasols and footmen laden with packages followed at a respectable distance, while children in tattered clothes darted among them, offering to hold horses, begging for coins.

"There!" Daphne cried, and Emily jumped. Following the line of her friend's finger, she saw a certain tall, russet-haired gentleman just coming out of Number 13.

"That's Gentleman Jackson's," Ariadne said. "You know, the Boxing Emporium where gentlemen go to learn *fisticuffs*." She whispered this knowingly, sitting at the very edge of the cushioned seat.

Emily found it hard to imagine Lord Robert taking a punch to the jaw, but perhaps he was quick enough that he did more of the punching himself. He certainly didn't seem any the worse for wear as he paused to tip his hat to a particularly pretty woman. Emily rapped on the panel overhead to get Mr. Phillips's attention and directed him to let them out at the next corner. But the moment they set their boots to the pavement, Daphne seized Emily and Ariadne by an arm and dragged them into the recessed doorway of a linen draper's shop.

"Priscilla," she hissed, "quick, or he'll see you!"

Priscilla slipped into the shadows with them. "Why are we hiding?" she asked as a group of young Hussars strolled by, the gold braid of their uniforms winking in the light. "The entire point of shopping on Bond Street is to see and be seen."

"The point in shopping today is to learn more about Lord Robert," Emily said. "Which will be a bit difficult in here."

"I cannot imagine why this works in books," Ariadne muttered, shifting to keep her elbow out of Emily's stomach. "It's quite uncomfortable."

"Well, I certainly don't want anyone to notice us following him," Daphne said. "I'd like a reputation as a lady." She paused to peer out. "Oh, it's all right. He's moved on."

They spilled back onto the pavement in time to see Lord Robert strolling south toward Conduit Street. Emily tugged down the edges of her midnight blue quilted jacket and smoothed the wrinkles from her softer blue gown. "I appreciate your zeal, Daphne, but as I do wish to speak to him, I rather have to let him see me."

Daphne blushed. "Sorry." She absently adjusted her green wool pelisse as well, stroking over the jade braiding of the long, fitted coat as if her hands needed something to do. Priscilla and Ariadne were also tweaking their pale muslin skirts or straightening a bit of lace across their shoulders. Anyone would think they'd come to speak to Lord Robert too!

With a shake of her head, Emily started after him. The sweet smell of baking cakes vied with the scent of lavender from the perfumery next door, but she fancied she smelled the tang of cloves over it all. Then she spotted him just ahead. He had stopped at a bow window and stood looking at the merchandise displayed therein. His head was cocked, as if whatever he contemplated required his complete concentration.

"That's Stedman and Vardon," Priscilla whispered over the rumble of passing carriages as the four of them ventured closer. "Jewelers to the aristocracy."

Ariadne sighed. "What if he's purchasing an engagement present for you, Emily?"

"He's wasting his time. At any formal function, I have to wear the Emerson emeralds, at least until my sister, Helena, produces an heir, who will then have to give them to *his* wife."

"Still," Daphne pressed, "it is rather romantic."

Emily had no time to comment, for Lord Robert seemed to have made up his mind. With a nod, he set off in the opposite direction. The girls had to hurry to keep up. Other shoppers exited in front of them, laden with packages, and they had to detour. A street urchin darted past, shouting, and they had to lift their skirts out of the way. The Hussars caught sight of Priscilla and converged, and that took a few moments to straighten out, leaving Priscilla with four calling cards and Daphne, to her amazement, with three.

By the time they caught sight of Lord Robert again, he was turning the corner onto Vigo Lane.

"Where is he going?" Ariadne panted, one hand on her straw bonnet, which was already a bit squashed from their time in the doorway and their confrontation with the soldiers.

"I don't know," Priscilla said just as breathlessly. "But if he continues at this pace, I shall expire on the pavement!"

"I have some lavender-sulfuric smelling salts," Daphne offered. She alone had no trouble keeping up, striding along with her muslin skirts flapping. "Lord Snedley highly recommends them after an exertion of a quarter mile or more."

Lord Snedley must have the constitution of a butterfly. But having a weak constitution certainly wasn't Lord Robert's problem. Emily even tried calling to him at one point, but she must have been too out of breath, for he didn't so much as turn.

In fact, he kept walking and walking, and Emily couldn't help but notice that they were straying ever farther from fashionable Bond Street. Soon the shops were narrower and darker, with no windows facing the avenue and far fewer shoppers. Ladies lounged in doorways, eyeing La Petite Four with narrowed eyes. Men in rough coats and heavy boots stalked past or, worse, stopped and stared.

One slouched up in front of them and held out a grimy hand.

"Penny for an old man?" the toothless fellow begged, his face even grimier than his hand.

Daphne began to open her reticule, but Priscilla snatched her hand and pulled her on.

"Do not show your money here," she whispered. "Emily, I think we should go back."

Ariadne was gazing about, wide-eyed. "No, this research is priceless."

"So is your virtue," Priscilla countered. "And I for one do not intend to lose it to a ruffian."

Up ahead, Lord Robert had just entered a shop. Emily could see the sign hanging above the door.

"Messiers and Sons," Ariadne read as they paused to catch their breath. "And see the diamond below? It's another jeweler."

"Odd place for a jeweler," Emily mused.

"It's a consignment shop," Priscilla said quietly. "People sell their jewels here when they have nothing left to sell, or change them to paste copies so no one will know they're destitute. Father's mentioned it."

So Emily had been right about the money. Perhaps Lord Robert's father had gambled away the funds. She couldn't see how Robert could have done so; surely his brother would have put a stop to it.

"We should go," she said, taking a step back. "Lord Robert won't want us to know his family's in such dire straits."

"Oh, the poor thing," Ariadne murmured. "To be blighted in his expectations. It's a classic plot."

And it explained his need to marry and soon, at that. Her dowry would come in very handy. But her father must have been aware of the Townsends' financial straits from the marriage settlements, so once again, she had nothing to use to convince him to break the engagement and let her attend the ball. Disappointment bit sharply. Could nothing go right?

Shoulders slumping, she turned with the others to go back the way they had come. Then she jerked to a stop.

Blocking their way was the toothless fellow who had begged for a penny earlier. His face was red and blotchy, his nose crossed with bulging veins. His shoulders were bunched under his tattered coat, and his fists were as big as hams.

"Spare a penny or two, love?" The request was more like a demand, and he shoved out his hand again, as if expecting obedience.

Daphne bumped into Ariadne in her haste to move away, and Priscilla clutched her reticule closer. That was not the way of it, Emily was certain. Bullies you had to face down.

"I'm afraid we have nothing for you," Emily said, forcing herself not to tremble. "Step aside and let us pass."

"Bossy 'lil thing, ain't you?" he grumbled, straightening and narrowing his eyes. "If yer such a fine lady, where's yer escort, then? Who's to stop me from taking what I want from any of you lot?"

"I am," a voice said behind him, and Emily caught her breath.

9

No Place for a Lady

The toothless behemoth swiveled, and there stood James Cropper behind him, feet planted and arms at the ready. He gave Emily his two-fingered salute before turning his frown on the fellow.

"Do as the lady says and step aside."

The creature easily had a stone's weight on Mr. Cropper, and she shuddered to think how his handsome face would look after it met those grimy fists. But to her surprise, the beggar ducked his head and shuffled his feet. "Didn't mean no 'arm, sir. 'Ow was I to know the lady was wif you?"

Mr. Cropper stepped forward. "I'll grant you you'll not meet her likes in the stews very often." He turned to Emily then and offered her his arm. "May I have the honor of escorting you home?"

He hadn't used her title or name, but she rather thought it was because the beggar was watching. In some places, a duke's daughter would fetch a high ransom, she'd heard. She truly didn't want the man to think she was without escort. But was she any safer with Mr. Cropper?

As if he guessed her concerns, his smile softened. The light in those remarkably fine gray eyes was as welcome as sunlight through the mist and warmed her just as gently. She put her hand on his arm. "The honor is all mine, sir."

"Sir, is it now?" the beggar chortled. "Since when does a lady walk with the likes of you?"

"When the lady is sufficiently gracious," Mr. Cropper said, leading her past him. "And so are her friends." His pointed look sent Priscilla, Daphne, and Ariadne scuttling in their wake. With a shake of his head, the beggar moved away.

Emily strolled along beside Mr. Cropper as if they were touring Hyde Park on a lovely spring afternoon, but she walked so close to him, her skirts brushed his brown trousers, and her gloved fingers seemed to want to curl around his strong arm and not let go. She cast him a quick glance, but he'd pulled his hat down lower over his eyes, and she couldn't catch a glimpse of them. She knew Priscilla must have found his brown wool coat lacking. Emily could not be so strict. He'd acted the part of hero, hadn't he?

But just when Emily was in complete charity with him, he sighed. "You shouldn't be here," he said, as if she hadn't realized it for herself. "This is no place for a lady."

Yet it was *his* place, she saw. He walked as if he owned the street. People came toward them, some of them bigger and darker than the beggar, and it took only a nod from him to send them packing. Not a few of them looked fearful as they did so.

"It appears you know it well," she said.

He laughed. "Oh, I'm no stranger to the stews. But you should be. Do you have any inkling of the danger you were in?"

She was beginning to get the general idea, but she didn't much appreciate the reminder. "While I acknowledge your help, sir, I cannot like your tone."

"No," he replied. "I imagine most people bow and scrape when they meet you. I'd rather save your life."

Ariadne had opened her reticule for her journal and pencil and was frantically scrawling as she walked.

"Do you truly think our lives were in danger?" Daphne put in, glancing around nervously.

"Four beautiful young ladies, wandering the streets with purses full of silver? What do you think?"

"Beautiful," Ariadne muttered.

"I don't recall Lord Snedley covering that," Daphne whispered to Priscilla.

"I told them this was foolish," Priscilla announced at full voice. "And I for one thank you for your gallant assistance, Mr. Cropper."

What was she doing? Emily had seen that look before, directed at any marriageable, titled gentleman who was so unlucky as to grace the front parlor at Barnsley. Priscilla was trying to attach Mr. Cropper's regard!

Emily's hand tightened on his arm. "I suppose," she allowed, "it was fortunate you happened upon us."

"It was difficult not to happen upon you," he said. "You were rather obvious, hurrying along behind Lord Robert."

"And just what are you doing here?" she asked, eyes narrowing.

He smiled. "Even a fellow like me can appreciate the sights of Bond Street, your ladyship."

His look made Emily's cheeks heat. Had she been right before? Was he following her? The air was suddenly too warm to breathe.

"And did you appreciate the sights at the Townsend town house as well?" she managed.

"The Townsend town house, your ladyship?"

He sounded so innocent, his face relaxed and open, but she knew it for an act. He ought to take a role in one of the plays Ariadne liked to write. Of course, very likely he'd have to play the villain.

"Yes. Do not deny you were there. I saw you, under the trees."

"Watching for me, were you?" he asked with a grin.

"I most certainly was not!"

"Oh, come now," Priscilla said. "You do seem to notice the fellow with alarming regularity."

Well, if that wasn't the pot calling the kettle black! How many times had Priscilla been swayed by a handsome face and a muscular arm? Just look at the Hussars this afternoon! If she didn't watch her step, she'd end up running off with a footman and forget all about finding a duke!

"It was not that I was watching you, Mr. Cropper," Emily said with a glare to Priscilla. "But as an artist, I notice when things are out of perspective."

"Yes, I heard you painted," he said, leaving Emily to wonder who had been gossiping about her. "And you're quite smart enough to have noticed that something's havey cavey with Lord Robert. However, I cannot like your methods. If you suspect him of something, you should notify the authorities."

"Suspect Lord Robert?" she asked, her pulse quickening once more in excitement. "Do you imply Lord Robert could be guilty of some crime?"

He raised his brows. "Were you following him for some other reason? Good Lord, you don't actually fancy the fellow!"

"For shame, sir," Daphne said. "He is her betrothed."

His jaw tightened, and he faced forward. "My condolences."

Emily stopped, forcing him to halt as well. "If you know something about him, sir, I demand that you speak plainly. As far as we've been able to tell, he is a gentleman."

"Which is why you chose to follow him all over London." His voice dripped with sarcasm. "Have a care, Lady Emily. He may just turn out to be a scoundrel after all. For everyone's sake, it would be better if you left the fellow alone."

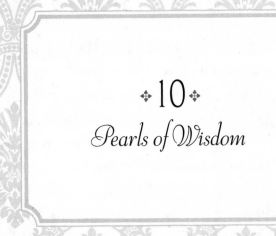

❖ 10 ❖

Pearls of Wisdom

James Cropper insisted on riding home with them to the Southwell town house and spent several moments in heated conversation with Warburton. When Mr. Cropper touched two fingers to his forehead in good-bye, Emily raised her chin and looked away. Priscilla nodded as if she were quite proud of her.

Warburton, however, was far less complimentary. "I hope Mr. Cropper was able to impress upon you the seriousness of your actions," he said, affixing them all with a hard-eyed look. "If your parents found out, Miss Tate, Misses Courdebas, I rather doubt they'd allow you all to visit Bond Street again."

Daphne and Ariadne hung their heads, and Priscilla's expressive green eyes filled with tears.

"We are sincerely sorry, Mr. Warburton," she said tremulously. "And we would be most grateful if you could find it in your heart not to tell our parents. Surely we should spare them such worry."

Ariadne began looking for her pencil.

Warburton gazed down at her. "I believe that can be arranged, Miss Tate. However, you must understand that London can be a dangerous place, whether you are on Bond Street or in Mayfair. Are you aware that a young lady from the Barnsley School was robbed the other day?"

If he had not had their attention before, he had it now.

"Who?" Priscilla demanded, tears evaporating.

"Miss Acantha Dalrymple. Her pearls were taken. Her father is most displeased, and her maid has been sacked for not paying sufficient attention to the jewel case."

"I'm very sorry for the maid," Priscilla said, "but I cannot be sorry for Miss Dalrymple. She flaunted those pearls at the least provocation. Is it any wonder she lost them?"

Daphne was bouncing up and down on her leather half boots, her green skirts billowing with each movement. "Oh, oh, but she didn't lose them in London! She lost them at Barnsley. While I was waiting for our carriage to be brought around, I heard her complaining."

Warburton raised his brows. "Interesting, but surely your headmistress would have investigated a theft at the school."

Most likely. Miss Martingale had strict notions of propriety. As, it appeared, did Warburton. "In exchange for not burdening your parents with news of your escapades," he said, "I will have your promises that you will not be so foolhardy again."

Of course, they all promised to be more careful. The butler's smooth face did not betray his feelings, but Emily thought by the quirk of his mouth that he was not entirely sure he believed them. "And as it appears that you lack ideas for appropriate activities for young ladies," he continued, "allow me to provide you with entertainment more fitting to your stations."

"Cleaning the attic!" Daphne moaned as they stared into the dark recesses atop the Southwell town house.

"We are not cleaning," Priscilla said, running a finger along the top of the nearest trunk and shuddering. "Maids clean. We are looking for gowns that might be useful to Emily as she debuts."

"If I debut," Emily reminded her. Her mood was nearly as dark as the shadows crowding the eaves, her thoughts as dry as the musty air. What was James Cropper doing? He followed them around and then had the audacity to claim that *she* was watching for *him*! While she had already admitted that his help had been welcome in facing down the beggar, he didn't have to escort them home and then tell Warburton, in excruciating detail no doubt, about their activities. James Cropper was nothing but an overweening tattletale!

"Are there any gowns up here?" Ariadne asked, poking at something tall, bulky, and draped in a white Holland cloth.

Emily shrugged. "Who knows? Do not mistake this for entertainment. Warburton was doing us no favor."

"Oh, I don't know," Daphne said, venturing deeper into the space. "Who knows what we might find." She raised the lantern Warburton had given them, and boxes, trunks, odd chairs, and mysterious shapes cast grotesque shadows in the golden light.

"The treasures of the ages," Ariadne intoned, lifting a gilded globe and giving it a spin. Dust flew out in all directions, and she sneezed.

"Better treasure than Acantha ever had," Priscilla said, bending over the trunk. "All I can say is that having someone steal her pearls is truly justice." She lifted the leather-strapped lid and made a face. "Old bed linens. Try that one."

Daphne obligingly hung the lantern on a hook overhead and went to bend over one of the larger trunks.

"But who would be so bold as to take them?" Ariadne mused, lifting another Holland cover and peering underneath. "Everyone we know is scared of her. Except for you, of course, Emily."

"Emily isn't afraid of anything," Daphne said, wrestling open the larger trunk nearest her. Her face brightened. "Oh, look, bonnets!"

Priscilla and Ariadne hurried over and peered down into the depths. Emily came more slowly. It was rather nice that her friends thought her so fearless, but at the moment, fear was beginning to gain a hold on her. What if they could find no fault to lay at Lord Robert's door, no reason to accuse him to His Grace? Would she actually have to marry the fellow?

The attic felt tight suddenly, the roof too low, the air too stuffy to breathe. Emily rubbed her hands up and down the sleeves of her soft wool gown, but the panic grew worse.

"Perfection," Priscilla declared. She pulled a bonnet from the tissue that had wrapped it and clapped it on Ariadne's head. "What do you think, Emily?"

The woven white reed cage wrapped about Ariadne's round face, dwarfing it. The four stuffed black birds on top stared out with a malevolent gleam in their amber glass eyes, and the twisted crimson fringe dangling at the bottom made Ariadne look as if her hair had caught on fire.

The sight of Ariadne in the fluffy bonnet melted Emily's panic and she started to giggle. "Very fetching. You should wear it to the ball."

Ariadne rolled her eyes and pulled it off. "No, thank you. I intend to pick my own gowns and bonnets. I'm sick to death of white muslin, white silk, white anything!"

"Lord Snedley advises it for young ladies in their first Season," Daphne explained. "As does Mother."

"Plain white passed out of fashion ages ago," Priscilla said, lifting her skirts to kneel before the trunk. "Simply tell your mother that Lord Snedley is mistaken."

Daphne gasped at the heresy, but Ariadne dropped her gaze, sighing. "It's much easier for me to write my thoughts than to speak them, Priscilla. Except with all of you, of course."

Priscilla sighed as well. "Then I suppose it's good that you have all of us to support you. Though I do think you could do with a bit of boldness." She laid aside the other bonnets and reached for the material they could see stored beneath.

"So long as you aren't as bold as Lord Robert," Daphne said, giving her sister's arm a squeeze, "and announce your engagement without having seen the fellow!"

"Now that's entirely too bold," Priscilla agreed. "And *this* is lovely." She pulled the gown from the trunk and laid it across her lap. The white gauze was threaded with gold, and tiny pearls dotted the bodice like new-fallen snow.

Emily took a step back, fingers going to her locket, as Priscilla rose and held the gown up.

"It looks as if it would fit you, and there's enough fabric that we could raise the line to be more in fashion." Priscilla frowned as if she'd noticed Emily's lack of enthusiasm. "Do not tell me you refuse light colors! This is gorgeous!"

Emily shook her head, throat tight. "It's my mother's. She wore it to Helena's come-out ball. I remember watching the fitting. Mother had two maids to help her because she was already coughing too much."

Priscilla reddened, then turned and laid the gown back in the trunk. "Well, then, we'll have none of that. You have entirely too much to be concerned about already."

Daphne put a hand on Emily's arm. "I know your mother would have wanted to see you at your come-out too."

Ariadne nodded, face pinched. Emily's entire body felt just as tight. She shook her head. "There's no point in wishing for the moon. His Grace obviously hoped I'd be presented as Lord Robert's wife, but I considered the ball my entrance into Society."

"So do I," Ariadne said. "At the dinner party Mother is hosting, I'll be nothing more than a pale copy of Daphne, like always."

"Only *you* see it that way," Daphne protested. "As if anyone would want to be a copy of me. I only hope Lord Snedley accepts his invitation to the ball that Priscilla sent to his publisher. I want to thank him for helping me become the lady I wish to be."

Ariadne bit her lip and looked away.

"That's why we must handle this mess with Lord Robert," Emily told them. "We all have reasons we need this ball to be a success. My entire future hinges on it, and we are no closer to solving that problem today than we were yesterday."

"Since *he* is so bold," Priscilla said, closing the trunk with a thud and rising, "then we must be bolder."

Ariadne's head jerked back around. "Oh, Priscilla, you do not know how right you are! Did we not just say that only someone that bold could have taken Acantha's pearls?"

Priscilla and Daphne stared at her. Emily did not trust the idea that was forming.

"Think on it," Ariadne pressed. "And did we not just see him where pearls might be sold?"

Priscilla rolled her eyes. "You are resorting to fancy again. He could have been selling some trinket he dislikes."

"No, she's right," Emily said, assurance growing. "Acantha was all set to steal him away from me, remember? He could have noticed those pearls; she was forever fingering them. He could have used his charm to get close to her, see where she stored them. And, in all the bustle of packing and graduation, how simple to slip away with them."

"He certainly reached London fast enough," Daphne mused.

"Quite as if he were running away," Ariadne agreed.

Priscilla put her hands on her hips. "And what about Mr. Cropper? He was at Barnsley too. Emily ran into him when we were trying to escape."

Emily felt her face heat as she remembered.

Daphne cocked her head. "Why was he at Barnsley? I've never seen him visit any of the girls, and he wasn't in the Grand Salon with the other guests."

"He cannot live in Somerset," Ariadne said with a frown. "Everyone we met along the way back to Bond Street seemed to know him. Surely London is his home."

"Precisely," Emily said, not certain why she felt so relieved. "So why go all the way to Somerset to steal pearls he could not have known existed?"

"Lord Robert could hardly have known Acantha's pearls existed either," Priscilla protested.

"But Lord Robert might have seen the opportunity and taken it," Emily replied. "And he had more need, what with his father gambling away the family fortune."

"You know what this means, don't you?" Ariadne said, blue eyes as bright as sapphires. When Daphne and Priscilla frowned, and Emily sucked in a breath, she leaned closer. "It means we have something against Lord Robert. Now all Emily must do is make him confess, and we'll have saved the ball!"

·11·
Stunned as a Statue

Emily tossed and turned all night. Could Lord Robert have really stolen Acantha Dalrymple's pearls or was she merely seeing treachery where she longed to find it? What if Priscilla was right and Mr. Cropper was the thief?

No, she could not make herself believe that. But neither did she believe she could make Lord Robert confess. She was ever too good at speaking her mind. Yet she knew she couldn't blurt out her suspicions. He'd either laugh them off or make up a clever story. Either way, she'd have lost her chance to gain any proof against him. Why couldn't she have more of Priscilla's finesse?

Emily thought and planned through the morning and was ready when Lord Robert arrived that afternoon. Mary had managed to tame Emily's curls inside a gray straw bonnet trimmed in rose velvet. Emily had dressed in her favorite gown, a gray-striped taffeta walking dress with a matching jacket. She liked the way it rustled as she moved, and she needed all the encouragement she could get, particularly as Lord Robert looked rather impressive in a blue coat of superfine wool and cream-colored trousers tucked in gleaming boots.

"Lady Emily," he said, bowing over her hand in the marble-tiled entry hall. "You look radiant, as always."

If he thought so, then she'd made the right choice in her attire. She smiled at him in what she hoped was an encouraging fashion. "It was very thoughtful of you to agree to escort me," she said as the footman held the red-lacquered door open for them and the cool air teased her cheek.

"Not at all," Lord Robert assured her, tucking her hand in his elbow and leading her down the stone stairs. "I realized that you might find my suit a bit sudden. I merely wanted to assure you that I will be a considerate husband."

Husband? Emily nearly choked just hearing the word. As they set off in the simple little carriage, Lord Robert at the reins and his groom behind, Emily knew she had to find her voice and a way to move the conversation toward pearls.

"The carriage certainly rolls along well," she tried as they passed the fine town houses of Mayfair. "Was it a recent purchase?"

Lord Robert was tipping his top hat to a group of ladies. He set it down rather quickly at Emily's question, his smile fading. "Yes, just this spring. I thought it more fitting than the fancier rig I drove before Father died."

The mention of his poor father was supposed to discourage her from asking any other questions, she supposed. That's what Lord Robert thought. "But you didn't use it at Barnsley, I gather," she said.

"Oh, no indeed. This sort of carriage is not designed for long journeys." He launched into such a detailed discussion of the merits of different types of coaches and the fine horses that pulled them, that Emily felt her eyes crossing. It wasn't until he exclaimed what a jewel the tilbury was that she found another opening.

"Speaking of jewels," she said, "I understand you're rather fond of pearls."

His brows went up so high, they disappeared under the curled brim of his top hat. "Pearls, Lady Emily?" For a moment, she thought she'd caught him. Then his mouth tilted up at one corner. "Is this your way of hinting at a betrothal present?"

Oh, but he was slippery, and oh, she wished her cheeks would cease heating! "Not in the slightest," she assured him, deciding to be bold. "I've heard entirely enough of pearls from a young lady at our school. Perhaps you know her, Acantha Dalrymple?"

His smile remained on his face, but as he gazed out over the horses she thought his hand tightened on the reins. "Yes, I believe we met at Barnsley. Charming young lady."

This time Emily did choke.

"Are you all right?" he asked, voice warm with concern.

When she waved him off, he reached out to pat her hand with his free one, his gloved fingers dwarfing hers. "Now, now, have no concern. She cannot replace you in my affections."

The fact that he thought Emily had affection for him and would actually see Acantha as a rival left her utterly speechless. She could only hope to do better when they arrived at Burlington House on Piccadilly, where the Marbles were stored. She was trying to decide if she should simply ask Lord Robert outright, when he escorted her through the public gates and into the yard.

And then she could say nothing for quite some time.

She'd read how the sculptures had arrived in England, what with Lord Elgin making off with them from their home in Greece, claiming a desire to protect them. The panels of creamy marble had once ranged along the walls of the Parthenon in far-off Athens, celebrating victories and festivals. Other statues and friezes had been brought to England to join them, so that everywhere she looked were horses and charioteers, gods and goddesses.

She could not see, however, how Lord Elgin had helped the marble sculptures. Instead of decorating the greening garden around her, the fine pieces were clustered around the coal shed in the rear yard of the palatial home as the current owner worked on remodeling. Even England's damp weather had taken its toll. Moss grew on fair skin. Soot darkened proud manes.

Yet still the lines were sleek, supple, stirring. The cool stone whispered of heroic battles, of pride and strength and courage. Standing beside them, Emily felt small. Her fingers strayed to her locket and gripped it tight. Surely she had it inside her to create something this profound, this moving.

She was so deep in thought that it was not until she and Lord Robert were on their way back to his carriage that she remembered she'd had another reason for this trip. She'd tried to be clever, she'd tried to be subtle, she'd tried to be bold. Perhaps she should just be herself.

"Why did you steal Acantha Dalrymple's pearls?" she asked.

Lord Robert pulled up short. "I beg your pardon?"

"Acantha Dalrymple," Emily pressed, refusing to be daunted, "the young lady you met at Barnsley. You stole her pearls."

His arm tensed under her hand. "Where on earth did you get that idea?"

With him regarding her so fixedly, she began to think she'd dreamed it. "You were at Barnsley," she insisted, "and we saw you yesterday enter the shop of a jeweler who's been known to accept consignment."

He frowned. "What were you doing in that part of London?"

She was not about to tell him. "It does not signify. What were you doing there if not selling the pearls?"

"Mother had some baubles she hoped to sell. The least I could do was spare her the trouble."

Plausible, but Emily felt as if some shape were missing from the picture he was painting, some color that would illuminate all if only she could discover it. "Then you have no financial troubles."

He snorted. "Hardly. But by all means, ask your father if you doubt me. His agents have been going over the marriage settlements. They know to the last penny what I bring to the marriage." He leaned closer, the scent of cloves wafting over her. "And I find it deeply troubling that you'd consider me such a cad, Lady Emily."

Oh, why did he always succeed in making her the villain? "But I hear you are a cad," she replied doggedly. "Will you also deny that you dallied with a merchant's daughter?"

She thought for a moment he would deny it. She could almost

see the thoughts churning behind those deep blue eyes. "I suppose it was too much to ask that the gossip not reach your tender ears," he said sadly. "I thought myself foolishly in love." He brought her hand to his lips. "That was, of course, before I ever met you again."

He knew more good lines than Ariadne!

This was no good. "You cannot be in love with me," she informed him. "You told my father we would wed before you'd so much as set eyes on me."

He pressed her hand. "And cannot duty lead to something more? At the very least a true friendship."

Friendship? Emily knew in her heart he was lying. There had to be some way she could catch him. Goodness, even Mr. Cropper thought him a criminal!

Her eyes narrowed. "Speaking of friendship, I met an acquaintance of yours the other day."

"Oh?" Lord Robert replied, releasing her hand.

Was that a hint of concern she heard in his voice? "Mr. James Cropper."

He froze. "Cropper? Cropper approached you?"

Not exactly, but Emily didn't care to explain how they'd met. "He came to see Father about some business."

"He spoke to your father?" She thought he was afraid, he turned so pale. What had she stumbled onto?

"No," she allowed, careful to keep the eagerness from her voice, "but that doesn't mean he won't the next time he calls."

A muscle was twitching in his jaw. "Is he the one who told you about the merchant's daughter? About the pearls?"

Emily frowned. "No. I merely heard gossip. Why does it matter who told me?"

He waved his free hand, face relaxing. "It doesn't, I suppose. I merely dislike seeing my good name blackened. Mr. Cropper is no gentleman, Emily, for all he likes to pretend otherwise. Do not trust him."

"I would be only too happy to comply, my lord," she said, watching him, "if you'd give me good reason."

His lips tightened, as if he refused to give her anything. "My request should be reason enough. I forbid you to have anything further to do with the fellow."

Lord Robert truly knew nothing about her if he thought *that* would work. "We must talk about this habit you have of forbidding me. It will not serve you well if we marry."

"*If* we marry?" He raised a brow. "Has nothing I've done convinced you that I am besotted?"

"If you are so pleased to be marrying me," she challenged, "so willing to please me in return, then why forbid me to attend the ball?"

He smiled, as if she'd given him a reprieve. "Is that what this is all about? I thought we'd settled that."

"We have." Despite herself, her chin was rising and with it her temper. "I will attend the ball."

He stiffened, and color flushed up his face. It seemed Lord

Robert had a temper as well. The realization must have shown on her face, for he hastily put on a smile as he led her toward the waiting carriage. "Well, then, I'll simply have to offer you something better, won't I?"

Emily cocked her head. "What could possibly be better than the magnificent ball we have planned?"

Lord Robert smiled at her. It was more genuine than the last, but it lacked his usual charm. "You'll just have to wait and see."

Wait? Oh, she would wait all right. Just long enough to beat him at his own game.

❖ 12 ❖

Forbidden Flirtations

As if Lord Robert's cryptic remark was not enough to keep Emily's mind busy, she returned home to find she had a caller.

"Mr. Cropper insisted on waiting for you," Warburton said. "I've sent for Mary."

Of course Emily could not receive him alone. She gave Warburton her jacket, then waited to follow him and Mary into the sitting room.

James stood as she entered, and she could not help noticing the contrast between him and Lord Robert. Lord Robert had been completely confident in himself and all he planned, his prestige as obvious as if the prince had knighted him in Westminister Abbey in front of London's finest. James was quieter, his brown coat and trousers less showy, yet the ornate red-and-gold sitting room felt smaller with him in it.

And she would never forget that smile. It seemed to promise her something quite grand if she'd just forget herself and . . . do what?

He bowed from where he stood before the dark marble fireplace. "Lady Emily, thank you for receiving me."

"Mr. Cropper," she said, inclining her head as she walked toward him. "I take it you are not here for His Grace this time."

"No, indeed. When I heard you were engaged to Lord Robert, I knew I'd lost that battle."

"You came to see His Grace about Lord Robert?" Emily took a step closer. "Why?"

"That's not really a subject for a fine lady like you."

Emily put her hands on her hips. "If you tell me that it is a matter between gentlemen, I will likely scream."

"Can't have that now, can we?" he said, rubbing a finger against his chin. "Perhaps I should get to the point. I've been thinking a great deal about you since our last visit."

He had? Oh, drat! There went her cheeks again!

As if suddenly realizing how she might take his words, he hurriedly added, "You do have a tendency to get into trouble."

Oh but he could be the most vexing man! Did he think her an infant that he must watch over her this way? His Grace certainly trusted her more than that! "I assure you," Emily replied with a toss of her curls that would have made Priscilla proud, "I can take care of myself."

"Oh, aye. You and your three friends were doing quite well when we met on Bond Street yesterday."

He *would* bring that up. "I already thanked you for that service, sir."

"Indeed you did, though rather grudgingly, I thought." He glanced at Mary, who was sitting on one of the plump red chairs in the corner sewing, trying to pretend she wasn't listening to every word, and Warburton standing against the red-and-gold wall as straight as a statue. As if deciding neither servant posed a problem, Mr. Cropper took a step closer to Emily. The scent of sandalwood drifted up, whispering of warm summer nights in exotic places. Emily blinked, trying to reconcile the cologne with the man who wore it.

"I wanted to assure myself that you heeded my warning," he murmured, gazing down into her eyes. "You've stayed away from the worst parts of London, haven't you?"

His gray eyes were fathomless, like looking up into the pale morning sky on a spring day. "Yes," she allowed. "Though I'd like to think I don't need a nursemaid."

"Oh, no," he replied, smile widening. "You've obviously out-grown the nursery."

She wished she had a fan. Priscilla said it was best used to rap insolent fellows across the knuckles. Emily would have preferred to wave it frantically in front of her heated face.

As if he sensed her discomfort, he straightened away from her. "Have you seen your fiancé recently?"

The question should have been casual, simply polite conversation, but Emily heard more behind it. He wasn't sure what Robert was about. Well, neither was she. She did think, however, that Mr. Cropper sounded just the wee bit vexed that she might have spent time alone with Lord Robert.

"I just returned from an outing with him," she replied, reaching up to play with her locket. "I mentioned your name. He didn't seem pleased to have made your acquaintance."

"No doubt," he said with a grin. "The feeling is mutual, I assure you."

"Why?" she demanded. "You both are so sure I should avoid the other, yet neither of you will explain."

"Perhaps it's not our place to tell," he said.

"That, sir, seems a handy excuse. Have you been following him? Is that why I keep running into you?"

"Perhaps we've merely been in the same neighborhoods."

"London has far too many neighborhoods for it to be a coincidence. And you and Lord Robert do not look as if you keep the same company."

He nodded. "And very likely wouldn't if we could. That's true enough."

Emily threw up her hands. "Can you say nothing of any use to me?"

"Only that you look very fetching in that gray gown."

The gown felt entirely too warm and tight. Emily shook her finger at him. "Charm will not save you, sir. I am immune to it. I swear that you and Lord Robert are a pair of coxcombs, entirely too full of yourselves to listen."

He laughed, a deep chuckle she was certain she'd find warming under other circumstances. "Well, I've been accused of that often enough."

"And have you been accused of theft, Mr. Cropper?"

She did not think he would answer honestly, no more so than Lord Robert had, but he pursed his lips as if giving the matter thought. "Can't say as I have, your ladyship."

"Perhaps it's merely that you're so good at evading capture,"

Emily suggested.

The smile didn't leave his face, drawing her closer. "Except by you," he pointed out. "You seem to find me even when I don't wish to be found. You're a rare woman, Lady Emily Southwell."

Heat flushed up her, and with it guilt. She should not have felt so warmed by his praise. "Thank you," she murmured, fingers going to her locket once more.

He cocked his head. "What's that you've got there?"

She cupped the oval with her hand, gazing down at the locket. She'd touched it so often, the gold was worn, its once bright sheen dulled. It was no less precious to her. "My mother left it to me so I wouldn't forget her."

His voice was soft. "You don't strike me as the sort who forgets someone she loves."

She shook her head. "I'm not. But after nine years, it's easy to forget little things, like the way she drank tea or combed out her hair." Her fingers were trembling, but she slid her nail under the edge and popped the locket open, turning it so he could see the miniature inside. "This is her."

He looked at the tiny painting, really looked, not like some people who glanced at a piece and pronounced it interesting. "You favor her, I think. You have her smile."

Emily felt her smile reappearing. "I like to think so." She glanced up to find him regarding her as if for the first time. She lowered her gaze and snapped the locket shut.

"I should go," he said, but he didn't move from her side.

He should indeed. She had so many things to do in the next five days: prove Lord Robert had stolen Acantha's pearls, finish her painting for the ball, determine what she should wear. But she couldn't make herself agree.

"Perhaps you'll answer me a question first," she heard herself say.

His eyes narrowed. "Likely it depends on the question."

Emily shook her head. "This should not be troublesome." She touched two fingers to her forehead in imitation of the salute he'd given her. "Why do you do this?"

He glanced down at his hand as if surprised she'd noticed. Meeting her gaze, he said, "It's an Irish gesture of respect."

"Are you Irish, Mr. Cropper?"

He grinned. "Sure-n I learnt the movement at me mother's knee, yer laidyship."

Emily could not help grinning back. "Well, it's quite charming."

"Oh, aye. Me mam is right proud of her Jamie, she is. Course the gesture gets a bit messy if I've been eat-n bread and jam. Can't figure how to keep them strawberries out of me hair."

She laughed. "You'd better stick with roasted chestnuts, then. You could hide any sign of them quite nicely."

"So long as they didn't singe me scalp."

"Oh, you needn't go so deep," she assured him. "You could put several of them right here, and no one would know." She wasn't sure what possessed her, but she reached up to touch the wave of hair over his forehead. The chestnut curl was warm and soft.

The laughter faded from his eyes, replaced by an intensity that took her breath away. Emily let her hand fall even as she heard Warburton cough from the doorway.

"And you," Jamie said softly, finger coming up to tweak the curls beside her ear, "you'd best not hide anything in that silky hair."

Emily couldn't move, couldn't breathe. Mr. Warburton seemed to have developed consumption, he coughed so hard.

Jamie leaned closer, and for an insane moment she thought he intended to kiss her. Even more insane was her reaction. She closed her eyes and wished Mr. Warburton to perdition.

"You're a fine woman, Lady Emily Southwell," Jamie murmured, his breath a caress against her cheek. "You should find yourself a fine man for a husband."

Something brushed against her temple, so soft she feared she had imagined it. It sent a tremor through her nonetheless. She opened her eyes, but Jamie was already striding for the door, which Warburton was holding wide for him, his gaze stern.

"Wait!" She took a step after him—to do what, she wasn't sure.

Jamie turned, and his smile was sad. "There's not much else can be said between us, my dear. But if you need me, you have only to look for me." He gave her his salute one last time and left.

"I'll see him out," Mr. Warburton said.

Emily stood in the middle of the room, feeling as if the space had grown cold without Jamie Cropper in it. Would he let her be so familiar as to call him Jamie? Did she dare to ask?

She rubbed her hands up and down her arms, the gown crinkling under her fingers. Mary regarded her with wide eyes, as if afraid Emily would turn into a goose and fly out the window. Emily felt just as concerned about her behavior.

She wasn't interested in courting just yet; she was going to spend her Season establishing herself as an artist. And if she were interested in courting, she certainly shouldn't be making eyes at a fellow like James Cropper. She was the daughter of a duke. He was a . . . well, she wasn't entirely certain what he was.

All she knew was that he was a cipher. One moment he was enforcing protection where she didn't need it, the next trying to steal a kiss. One moment she wanted to shout at him, the next to kiss him back. All while she was engaged to Lord Robert!

Did anyone on earth understand this business with boys?

❖ 13 ❖
They're All Mad!

"The first thing you must know about boys," Priscilla said later that afternoon, "is that they are all mad."

Emily could easily believe *that* as she sat across from Priscilla in the sitting room of the tiny house in a forgotten corner of Mayfair—the only house, it appeared, Priscilla's father had been able to afford. The little room was far less opulent than the sitting room at His Grace's town house. The furniture looked as if it had been picked from a number of rooms and thrown all together, with less than pleasing results.

"Completely illogical," Priscilla continued, fingers curling around the worn gilt ends of her chair arm, which were shaped like lions' heads. "Look at Lord Brentfield. What on earth would possess him to marry Miss Alexander of all people?"

"I like to think it was her art that impressed him," Emily said, from her own chair, which was covered in scarlet ostrich plumes. "She's very good, you know."

Priscilla rolled her eyes. "A gentleman is seldom as impressed by a lady's accomplishments as he is by her anatomy."

Emily sighed. "I certainly hope you're wrong, or I'm doomed, Pris."

"No, you're not," Priscilla said immediately, straightening so that the pink satin ribbons decorating the front of her gown tumbled freely down the graceful skirt. "Because the only thing more impressive to a gentleman than a lady's anatomy is her connections. You are the daughter of a duke, you know."

"So you think that's all Lord Robert cares about?" Emily rolled her eyes. "Perhaps your father can adopt me in time for me to attend the ball."

Instead of laughing, Priscilla's look darkened. "You do not wish to be a member of my family right now. Trust me on that score."

Emily lowered her voice and glanced toward the door, where Mrs. Tate had only recently exited. "Are things still so bad?"

"Impossible," Priscilla whispered back. "Mother keeps insisting that only the attendance of the Prince Regent at the ball will save us from disaster."

"I doubt the prince will be much help," Emily whispered back. "You'll have better luck with your duke, whoever he may be!"

Priscilla brightened, but her smile lasted only long enough for her mother to return to the sitting room. Trailing behind Mrs. Tate and simpering obsequiously were Acantha Dalrymple and her mother.

Mrs. Dalrymple looked nothing like her daughter. Where Acantha was narrow and dark, as if even her physical nature were stingy, Mrs. Dalrymple was the epitome of overblown satisfaction. Her ample girth was encased in a stylish cambric gown of pale yellow. Her bonnet groaned under the weight of peacock feathers, silk sunflowers, and green satin ribbon. With her short quilted jacket of a deeper yellow, she resembled nothing so much as an overripe melon.

Though Mr. Dalrymple's father had made his fortune in trade and the family had only recently joined the ranks of the Beau Monde, Mrs. Tate acted as if royalty had come to call. She fluttered about, fingers darting from the soft pleats of her blue day dress to the dark curls beside her slender face. To Emily, who'd visited often over the years, Priscilla's mother had always seemed rather bemused that she'd birthed someone as breathtaking as Priscilla. Now she couldn't seem to believe she'd been visited by people as impressive as the Dalrymples.

Mrs. Dalrymple seated herself on the flowered settee beside Priscilla's mother, leaving Acantha to take up a spindle-backed chair next to Priscilla and Emily. Her gown was a wondrous creation of fine blue cambric and silk lace, with a ruffled skirt and graceful sleeves that danced when she moved her gloved hands. It would have been a lovely dress, on a more lovely creature. Emily thought she heard Priscilla sigh in envy as she gazed on the paisley shawl that draped Acantha's bony shoulders. Acantha merely smiled beatifically.

"And are you enjoying your Season, Miss Dalrymple?" Priscilla's mother asked after they were all settled.

Acantha dropped her gaze demurely. "Oh, a very great deal, Mrs. Tate. Everyone has been so kind, so gracious."

"I declare our sitting room is never void of callers," Mrs. Dalrymple said with a proud smile at her daughter.

Acantha shot Priscilla and Emily a look. "Yes, even Lord Robert Townsend. We met when he was at Barnsley, and now he calls most every day."

Emily stiffened. How dare Acantha imply that Emily's fiancé was more fascinated with *her*! Not that Emily was in any way enamored with Lord Robert. But still!

Priscilla must have been of the same mind, for she winked at Emily. "Oh, how delightful," she told Acantha. "I'm certain the two of you get on famously."

Acantha blinked as if she had not expected so enthusiastic a response. Then she stroked her lovely shawl, and Priscilla's gaze followed each movement.

"Indeed we do," Acantha said. "Such a fine gentleman. He has the very best taste, in clothing, in furnishings. He was most admiring of my pearls."

Of course he had been! He'd very likely stolen them from under that smug little smile.

As the two mothers turned to discussing the latest news of the war, Priscilla smiled at Acantha. "Such a shame you lost your pearls," Priscilla said, just loud enough that the mother's couldn't hear.

Acantha's expression was nearly as poisoned. "But I didn't lose them. I found them later, in the drawer of my dressing table."

Now Emily blinked. "What?"

As Priscilla frowned, Acantha nodded. "It's true. It seems I'd only misplaced them."

But if the pearls weren't missing, then Lord Robert could not be a jewel thief. Oh, why had she thought they'd uncovered his secret?! He was obviously far more cunning than they'd guessed. So, if not the pearls, then what?

"It seems you've been quite fortunate," Priscilla said to Acantha, but each word was bitten off as if she didn't appreciate being in a position to praise the creature for anything.

Acantha fluffed at the limp brown curls on one side of her narrow face. "Too true. Fortune seems to follow me, just as it does my dear Papa. Of course, I am entirely too gracious to lord it over anyone, particularly someone of your dire straits, Miss Tate." Her dark gaze roamed over the mismatched furniture and common paintings of the sitting room, and she scrunched up her long nose in obvious distaste.

Priscilla's fingers were pressed so deeply into the lion's mouth of the armrest that Emily wouldn't have been surprised to hear the wooden beast gag. Why couldn't Acantha leave well enough alone? If Emily had been home, she'd have called for Warburton to throw the creature out, but as this was Priscilla's home, all Emily could do was sit and try not to do or say anything that would bring shame on Priscilla, the Tates, or His Grace. Miss Martingale said that the daughter of a duke would sit serenely while her fate was pronounced by the executioner.

Sometimes Emily hated being the daughter of a duke.

"Yes, I am, by nature, entirely too sensitive," Acantha said now with a sigh, as if she bore a burden too great for her scrawny frame. "I care too deeply what others think and feel. In fact, I'm likely the only one who understands how devastated Lord Robert feels after the tragic accident."

Emily started. Accident? She opened her mouth to ask and felt Priscilla's slipper come down hard on her own.

"Well," Priscilla said, "that was most kind of you. I suppose the fellow needed someone to comfort him. Don't you agree, Emily?"

Emily met her green gaze, feeling a bit as if she were walking out onto an empty field with no knowledge of how she'd come to be there in the first place. "Oh, indeed," she tried.

It must have been a good enough answer, for Priscilla nodded. "And then compounded with the death of his poor father. Well . . ."

"Actually, his father died first," Acantha corrected her with a sniff of disdain at Priscilla's apparent ignorance. "Though I'm sure Lavinia Haversham's death hit much harder. Robert thought himself in love, after all." She squealed out one of her laughs, and both mothers glanced at the girls. Mrs. Tate's ruby lips were parted, as if she wasn't sure whether to speak. Mrs. Dalrymple's dark brows were drawn down over her heavy nose as if she suspected Acantha's laugh was misplaced.

Acantha favored her mother with a sickly smile that was no doubt meant to be reassuring and leaned closer to Emily and Pricilla. "Yes, Lord Robert thought himself foolishly in love. That was before he met me, of course."

He'd said very nearly the same thing to Emily! That could only mean one thing: this Lavinia Haversham Acantha was talking about was the merchant's daughter with whom Lord Robert had dallied.

"It didn't matter if Lord Robert was in love," Emily told Acantha as the mothers returned to their own conversation. "His family would never have allowed him to marry a merchant's daughter. Particularly one ill enough to die so young."

"Ill?" Acantha rolled her eyes. "You two are sadly misinformed. Lavinia Haversham was never ill. Indeed, she went everywhere with Lord Robert. Several balls, Astley's Riding Amphitheatre, the Egyptian Hall, Lord Elgin's Marbles . . ."

The Marbles! But Emily had had to beg him to take her there! And he hadn't offered to take her anywhere else. Besides, he wouldn't let her attend a single ball.

"He might even have offered for her," Acantha insisted, "if she hadn't died. Can you imagine anything worse than dying by accident in your first Season? She passed on only four days before we graduated, you know."

"No," Priscilla said, "we didn't know. And I do believe you're making this all up."

Emily couldn't tell whether the tragic story of Lord Robert's relationship with Miss Haversham was true or not. For all his claims of grief over his father and the girl he said he loved, Lord Robert had a poor way of showing it. Dallying with a married woman? Agreeing to marry Emily less than a day after Miss Haversham had had her accident? For he could not have taken longer and still reached Barnsley in time for graduation.

And what of the marriage settlements? His Grace had said they'd been working on the things for months. So had Lord Robert dallied with Lavinia Haversham *knowing* he was going to marry Emily instead? Any way she looked at it, Lord Robert was an unconscionable scoundrel.

Acantha apparently thought otherwise, as her gaze darkened. "I did not make it up! I have exquisite details from the gentleman himself." She glanced at her mother, then rose, lowering her voice. "Take a turn about the room with me, and I shall tell you all."

✤ 14 ✤

*Crisp Cotton
and Chamomile*

Emily was quite glad Priscilla, Daphne, and Ariadne had scheduled fittings for their ball gowns the next day, for it gave the four of them an excuse to meet and discuss Acantha's strange tale. Not to mention, it allowed Emily to escape the house again. She merely told Warburton that Priscilla had requested her company. She didn't tell him Priscilla had requested her advice on the ball gown. Sadly, he would never have believed her.

Of course, Emily was not being fitted. Everyone thought she was still to be married. Even her father. She'd tried broaching the matter to His Grace the previous evening. He'd been home and in his study for all of a quarter of an hour before changing for dinner with the Home Secretary.

"I am hearing distressing rumors about Lord Robert," she had tried when her father noticed her standing in the doorway and asked her what was wrong.

His smile was kind. "I imagine any young man of Lord Robert's expectations engenders some amount of envious gossip."

Emily moved closer to where he stood behind the massive, claw-foot desk. Parchment was neatly stacked here and there across the polished top, and he seemed to be taking a moment to study each piece before laying it back down again.

"I explained to him my desire to join the Royal Society this Season," she told His Grace, "to exhibit my paintings. He did not seem encouraging."

He frowned, but she could not tell whether it was from concern over what she'd said or concern over what was on the paper in his hand. He did not look up. "Lord Robert is under a great deal of pressure from his family. I imagine that's what's driving his desire to marry so quickly."

Emily bent her head to try to peer up under his gaze. "Could you not persuade them to wait?"

He sighed and let the paper fall. "I would prefer not to, Emily Rose. These are trying times. We thought the threat to England vanquished, yet he manages to raise an army and rally France into a furor once more."

He, Napoleon. She should have known it was not her marriage that had brought her father back so soon from Vienna. He had important duties, for the Crown, for England.

His Grace looked up and met her gaze, brown eyes solemn. "I want you safely settled, Emily. Your mother and I both wanted this match. I know she'd be very proud of you."

Emily had nodded and left. Truly, what else could she do? It wasn't as if she could appeal to her mother for help. The very idea just made her feel hot, angry, ready to throw something.

But that wouldn't have helped matters either.

Now she stood at the back of Madam Levasard's, watching as Priscilla and Daphne took turns on the raised platform so that the seamstresses could tuck and pin and stitch them into their gowns. The shop was light and airy, with bolts of fine fabric clustered along the walls, lace dripping from wooden wheels, and fine feathers waving from drying racks. Half-finished gowns hung here and there, tantalizing the imagination. The air smelled of crisp cotton and the chamomile tea that Madam was so fond of serving. Indeed, Priscilla's mother and Daphne and Ariadne's mother, Lady Rollings, were already seated by the front window with steaming cups in front of them, waiting to critique the final gowns.

"So who exactly is Lavinia Haversham?" Daphne asked as if she had not been able to follow Emily's and Priscilla's explanations. She was taking her turn on the platform, a seamstress kneeling at her feet to let out the hem of the dazzling white gown.

"That wealthy merchant's daughter who dallied with Lord Robert," Ariadne offered, thumbing through some of Madam's sketches and pausing on one of a daring green gown with a sigh. "Though I would have made her a princess, mind you, with a name like Scheherazade or Alamahari."

"She was not a member of Good Society," Priscilla explained, eyeing the delphinium blue fabric that had draped her only moments before, "but Lavinia's father hoped to buy her way into the Beau Monde with a titled husband. That should not have been difficult. Acantha related that Miss Haversham was beautiful, gracious, and kind. If she hadn't slipped in her bedchamber, struck her head on the corner of her dressing table, and expired,

Lord Robert might well have defied his family and married her."

"Perhaps not," Daphne put in hopefully. "Perhaps he realized that Lady Emily had always been his one true love." She gave Emily a look out of the corners of her eyes.

Certainly Lord Robert wanted Emily to think that. She still couldn't make herself believe it. "And perhaps pigs might fly," she replied.

Priscilla nodded. "His behavior is shameful. It's as if he simply forgot all about Miss Haversham and went happily on with his life. Doesn't the poor girl deserve better?"

Ariadne and Daphne were nodding as well. Emily could not look at them. She gazed down at her gloved fingers, so tightly entwined in front of her that she could feel all her bones.

"Sometimes," she said, "it's easier to forget, to pretend you never knew the person you loved."

Someone, likely Daphne, sucked in a breath. Emily managed to look up. They were all regarding her as if she were made of fine crystal, and if they touched her, she might break. Even the seamstress paused to stare at her.

"I simply meant," she said, wanting to hide under the little wire-backed chair, "that there might be a reason for him rushing off to Somerset to meet me, why he doesn't speak much of her."

"I suppose his heart may be broken," Daphne conceded. Then she turned so the seamstress could work on her graceful train.

Priscilla shook her head. "I'm not willing to agree that he has a heart. Acantha said Miss Haversham's family has retired to the country for the remainder of the Season to mourn. Should he not mourn as well?"

It did seem rather heartless. Was this all some game to him? Would he treat Emily the same way? Was he pretending to court her, only to dash her hopes at the last second? If so, he was toying with the wrong person. One did not abandon the daughter of a duke!

"I can't understand him," Emily said. "As much as it pains me to admit, however, this sad tale doesn't help us in the slightest."

"Surely His Grace would be moved by it," Daphne protested, scooping up her train. The seamstress rose, held out her hand, and helped Daphne off the platform to go show Lady Rollings.

"Very likely he would find it tragic," Emily replied as they passed. "However, while it does not reflect well on Lord Robert, we have nothing to lay at his door except extremely shallow feelings, especially as we now know that he did not steal Acantha's pearls."

"Then what do we do?" Priscilla exclaimed. "You cannot give up! We could never be happy knowing you were consigned to that shallow fellow! Besides, think about the ball, Emily—roses, fairies, goldfish!"

"Perhaps you could just tell Lord Robert you wish it above all things," Ariadne suggested, rummaging through the rose-colored folds of her reticule.

"I told him so yesterday," Emily replied. "He said he would simply have to make me a better offer."

"I knew it," Ariadne said, head rising and eyes lighting. "He *is* smuggling virgins. I read a pamphlet on it. They were handed out at Hatchards Lending Library."

"Next time," Priscilla advised, with a smile and a shake of her head, "go into the library instead of loitering out front to see the gentlemen passing. Lord Robert is definitely *not* smuggling virgins."

"I don't see why not," Ariadne said with a sniff. "He has the connections, and what virgin would deny him anything?" She blushed furiously.

"I don't think Lord Robert smuggles young ladies of quality, or anything else," Emily said quickly as Ariadne opened her mouth to protest. "And, as Acantha's pearls were found, it appears he isn't a jewel thief either."

"Perhaps Acantha is lying," Ariadne said, as if she couldn't bear to see another theory proved wrong. She pulled a smaller sack from her reticule and set it down on the sketch of the green gown.

"Unfortunately, no," Priscilla said. "She was entirely too smug about the matter."

"I still say he's up to something," Ariadne insisted.

"I agree," Emily said. "But what?"

"Perhaps you should discuss the matter with His Grace," Daphne put in, returning to their sides. "Lord Snedley advises that honesty is the best policy in all things, except when answering the question 'Does this gown show I've eaten a dozen cakes in the last fortnight?' of course." She turned to Ariadne. "Mother wants to see your gown now."

Ariadne waved a hand. "The one she picked out for me looks

just like yours, only without the shimmery overskirt. Who needs to see it again?" She turned to Emily. "Daphne's right. Speak to His Grace."

Emily shook her head. "I spoke with him last night. He at least intends well by me. He truly believes this marriage will keep me safe. No, I can only go to him when we have something tangible."

Ariadne's smile formed, widening her round cheeks. "Then we are still investigating Lord Robert?"

"Yes," Emily said, lowering her voice and beckoning them closer, "but I think we must narrow our purpose. Mr. Cropper thinks him a criminal, and Acantha Dalrymple thinks him a saint. We have far too many rumors about Lord Robert. We must seek the truth from the man himself. If Acantha is lying, and he is a jewel thief, it may be that he will steal something else. If not, he may show us the truth behind his strange actions. Tomorrow, we shall follow him again, and this time, we won't stop until we learn his secret!"

❖ 15 ❖
Art and Artifice

As if Lord Robert knew they were determined to thwart him, he called on Emily that very afternoon. She was all set to have Warburton turn him away, until she learned he'd brought an acquaintance.

"Lady Honoria St. Gregory," Warburton intoned as he ushered the lady and Lord Robert into the sitting room. Emily was thoroughly sorry for the gown she'd worn. It was a ruffled pink silk day dress her father had had made for her. She'd hoped she'd spill enough paint on it that she wouldn't feel guilty giving the thing to the rag man. But painting had once again proven difficult, and the gown had won over *The War of the Roses.*

"I have been telling Lady St. Gregory all about your work," Lord Robert explained after they had been seated in the claw-footed chairs near the fire.

Lady St. Gregory was already glancing about at the battle scenes. She was younger than Emily had expected, perhaps only ten years Emily's senior. Her glossy black hair was swept back from a high-cheekboned face; her gaze was as icy blue as the short jacket and matching gown she wore. Her soft pink lips somehow managed to convey her feelings better than the rest of her calm face. As Lady St. Gregory's lips thinned, Emily gathered with a sinking heart that the sculptress was not exactly pleased with what she saw.

"It's a pleasure to make your acquaintance," Emily said politely. "I've followed your work in the newspapers."

"Yes, *The Times* in particular has been kind to me," the lady acknowledged. She did not so much as lean back in the chair, sitting as ramrod straight as Miss Martingale always said a lady should sit. Miss Martingale would have adored Lady St. Gregory: the graceful way she held her gloved hands, the elegant tilt to her chin, the way her embroidered slippers just crossed at the ankles below her blue hem, which had no ruffles whatsoever.

"And what made you decide upon battle scenes?" she asked.

"Yes, that was a bit odd," Lord Robert agreed. "Though mind you, I think they're heavenly."

Emily kept the smile on her face. "I believe we should remember history and honor those who went before. That's why I also paint myths and the deaths of great leaders."

Those lips did not warm in the slightest, not even in understanding. "Historical epics. They were all the rage a few years ago."

She made it sound as if Emily were hopelessly behind the times or blindly following a path laid out by others more talented. Emily swallowed. "I believe an artist should paint what moves her, my lady."

Lady St. Gregory inclined her head. "I quite agree. Why do I find it difficult to believe that battle scenes and deaths move a young lady of your limited years?"

Emily felt as if she would explode like one of the shells in her battle scenes. She squeezed her knees together to keep from rising, and the ruffles bunched against her shins.

"Perhaps because you do not know me well," she said with as much civility as she could manage, fingers clutching her locket. "I assure you, I care passionately about the scenes I paint."

"No doubt," Lady St. Gregory said.

Why had Emily thought she would have anything in common with this icicle of a woman? There was no sensibility, no generosity of spirit. Lady St. Gregory very likely sculpted the stone by gazing at it in so withering a manner.

"I care so much, in fact," Emily continued, "that I was hoping to exhibit one of my paintings at Priscilla Tate's come-out ball. Perhaps that piece will give you a better idea of what I've learned."

Lady St. Gregory frowned. "But Lord Robert tells me you may not be attending the ball after all."

"Lord Robert is mistaken," Emily said, glaring at him.

He had the good sense to look embarrassed. "Lady Emily is devoted to her craft," he said to Lady St. Gregory. "I know how much she wants to impress you. As she cannot attend the ball, I thought perhaps you could view her work today. Surely you can see the genius in it."

Emily felt her gaze softening. Did he truly understand what her painting meant to her, how much she longed to join the Royal Society? Had he sought out the sculptress simply to help Emily reach her dreams? No one had ever done anything of such magnitude for her before.

How very odd that it should be Lord Robert. Was this some-how part of his deceptions? What would it profit him? She had no time for these questions now, not when her future sat so sternly across from her!

"I can see that Lady Emily is talented," Lady St. Gregory allowed. "I simply question her range."

Range? What was that supposed to mean? She'd done battles at sea, battles on land, mythical battles in the air! What more did the woman want?

"I find the pieces quite realistic," Lord Robert argued, "for all my dear Emily has never been to war. The horse in that one has a partic-ularly mean look to it." He shivered. "I'd not wish to meet its like."

He was not helping the situation. Emily was tempted to ask him to wait in the library. She didn't need another witness to her flogging.

"I find no fault in the execution of the pieces," Lady St. Gregory assured him, "but she is quite correct, Lord Robert. I do not know her." She leveled her cool gaze on Emily, and Emily had to fight not to squirm under it. "One of the things about great art is that one can learn something of the artist by looking at the cre-ation. I see little of you in these."

She could not have felt worse if Lady St. Gregory had slapped her. "I'm not entirely sure what you mean, my lady."

Lady St. Gregory's smile was tight. "I'm sure you don't." She rose. "It was a pleasure meeting you, Lady Emily. If you exhibit at Miss Tate's ball, please send me word. Otherwise, I wish you luck in your marriage. You need not escort me, Lord Robert. I have other calls to make."

No doubt to spread her joy. Emily could only manage a nod as the woman left.

Lord Robert, standing and watching Lady St. Gregory leave, shook his head. "My, that did not go well."

"No, it did not." Emily slumped in her seat, feeling as if even her bones had wilted. Was she truly such a terrible artist? Had she never managed to create a piece that spoke to others?

Lord Robert came to sit beside her, his face soft and forlorn. "Now, now," he said, reaching out to pat her hand. "Perhaps it is best to know the truth."

Emily nodded miserably. "I suppose so. Yet I was so sure I was ready for the Royal Society."

"It is all too easy to delude oneself when one cares as deeply as you do," Lord Robert said. "But now that you know, you can follow a different path."

Follow a different path? Stop painting? She could as easily stop breathing! She forced her bones to straighten, her head to rise. "No, I must keep trying. If my efforts are lacking, I must learn to do better."

"How brave you are," Lord Robert murmured. His finger grazed her cheek, and she felt as if he were tracing a pattern inside her. "Most people would surrender after such a set down."

No, she would hear no word of giving up. "But I can't. Don't you see?" She waved a hand around at all her battle scenes, feeling as if she'd been forced to go to war as well. "This, these paintings, my art, it's who I am, Robert. Fate made me the daughter of a duke, but in my heart, I'm an artist."

He gathered her close, and Emily stiffened. What was he doing? But before she could demand an explanation, he rested his head against hers. "I know you're an artist, Emily," he murmured. "You've painted your likeness on my heart, and I am awed by its beauty."

How could he of all people know exactly the right words to say at that moment? He was supposed to be a scoundrel! Yet she could not help the warmth that stole over her, the desire to hug him close and swear to renew the fight. His large hand came up to rub her back in lazy circles. The feeling was surprisingly pleasant.

She let her head fall to his shoulder as she sat cradled in his embrace. Perhaps he was right. Perhaps her work was enough. At the moment, she couldn't remember why she'd wanted to join the Royal Society so badly.

What was she thinking? What was she doing?! Emily yanked herself out of his arms and stood on shaking legs. He gazed up at her, brows raised, eyes warm. He seemed to expect her to pledge her undying devotion.

And what was she to say? She knew where her devotion lay. The Royal Society was waiting, ready to recognize her as they had other accomplished artists among the aristocracy. Artists of the Royal Society were patronized by the queen and the royal princesses, the works admired far and wide. She would be the most fortunate of mortals if she were allowed to join them.

"Thank you for bringing Lady St. Gregory," she told Lord Robert. "It was most kind of you. I'm sure you understand when I say you've given me much to think about."

He rose, smile soft, as if he knew the storm that raged inside her. "Of course. But I shall see you the day after tomorrow, at our engagement dinner. We'll be signing the settlement papers then."

His tone was firm, and she knew she should agree. Once she signed those papers, she was as good as married. There'd be no crying off, not unless he *did* turn out to be something altogether horrid like a jewel thief or virgin smuggler. But at the moment, all Emily could give him was a nod. He seemed to accept that, for he offered her a bow and went to the door.

As soon as he was gone, Emily collapsed onto the nearest chair. Why was he being so nice? He'd forgotten to mourn his own father, dismissed the woman he loved with no more thought than he'd give the morning's tepid tea. Why encourage *her*? Why help her? Could it be that Lord Robert felt something for her after all?

As it was, Emily's feelings were as jumbled as an upset paint box. How wonderful to think someone cared as much about her painting as she did! How noble that he'd tried to find a compromise that allowed her to keep her dreams. How ridiculous that the best he could find to praise in her work was the nasty look on a horse's face! How horrid that Lady St. Gregory of all people could see nothing more.

But Emily had to show her more! The ball was her last chance. Lady St. Gregory would never be convinced to return to the town house now. Emily had to create the perfect painting, a feast for the eyes, the epitome of beauty and grace, and all within the next four days!

Unfortunately, for any of that to happen, she must also prove Lord Robert Townsend a criminal, once and for all. She just hoped he really was a criminal and not simply out to steal her heart.

·16·
The Frill of the Chase

La Petite Four began their quest the next morning, but they had to wait an inordinate amount of time for Lord Robert to get up. Emily finally sighted him through the crack in the shutters on Priscilla's carriage window, as the coach stood parked just down the square from the Townsends.

"He's coming out the door," she said to the others seated around her.

As Daphne smothered a squeal, Priscilla rapped on the wooden panel above their heads. A moment later, the panel was slid aside, and the florid face of her family coachman appeared.

"You know what to do, Mr. Wells," Priscilla said.

"Yes, miss." He shut the panel; the coach moved forward.

"What will we do if he notices us?" Ariadne whispered as if Lord Robert were standing just outside the door.

"He *won't*," Emily predicted. "How many brown carriages are there in London with unremarkable horses?" She glanced at Priscilla. "Sorry, Pris. You know what I mean."

"That's the first time," Priscilla replied with a grin, "I've ever considered it a blessing."

It was a considerable blessing. The way Lord Robert felt about carriages, he would have easily recognized His Grace's with its ducal arms emblazoned on the door. He would certainly have noticed the pair of perfectly matched black horses Daphne and Ariadne's father used to pull their carriage. Priscilla's rather drab equipage blended right in. And it wasn't a tilbury.

Emily was also grateful that the Tates had been persuaded to let La Petite Four go for a drive together, without Mary or any other companionship other than Mr. Wells. Priscilla had convinced her parents that Lady Emily was pining away inside her house all alone and wanted to see more of the grand city. No one would get out, chase gentlemen about London, or in any other way contribute to a scandal.

At least, not yet. Thank goodness Priscilla's coachman was up for a lark and impressed enough by His Grace's title to do their bidding. Daphne, unfortunately, was less willing.

"I will not follow him on foot," she said, sitting back on the worn leather seats and crossing her arms over the black satin edging on her yellow short jacket. "Lord Snedley says that St. James's is the hunting grounds of the gentleman about town. I refuse to be the prey. Especially not after what happened last time, with the canine."

Ariadne toyed with the silk fringe on her shawl. "I think Lord Snedley simply meant that a number of gentlemen might be found on St. James's. That's where White's is, you know."

And that's where Lord Robert was heading. They all took turns peering out the windows at the famous gentleman's club as Robert's coach approached it, with theirs not far behind. The neat white building with its black shutters boasted a bow window over-looking the street.

"I've read that Beau Brummell and his friends sit there and comment on the ladies passing," Ariadne confided.

"And you cannot tell me," Priscilla said, "that the ladies don't know it."

"What do you think he'd say about us?" Daphne asked.

Emily wasn't sure she wanted to know what the most notorious fashion arbiter of their time would say about her. She'd heard he'd once required a gentleman to change his cravat fifty-seven times before the Beau was satisfied with the tie of the neck cloth. She was glad they were safely anonymous in Priscilla's carriage.

"He's leaving again," Priscilla reported from the window a short time later. "And he's on foot this time." She turned to look at Daphne. "Someone better go after him."

Daphne threw up her hands. "Oh, very well. I suppose it's not so bad during the morning. Come along, Ariadne. I need a chaperone."

"If we do this again," Priscilla told Emily as the door closed behind them, "we must find disguises."

"I brought my evening cloak," Emily replied, "but it's not much help in the daylight. Mary told me her sister works for an actress. She'd probably know what to do."

They speculated on which actress it might be, then lapsed into silence. Emily rubbed her gloved finger against the dark wood panel of the door. She'd been trying to think of a way to mention Lord Robert's perplexing behavior from the day before, but somehow she hadn't been able to bring up the matter in front of Daphne and Ariadne. Perhaps it was best just to state the matter.

"Lord Robert took me into his embrace yesterday," she said, glancing up in time to see Priscilla's emerald eyes widen.

Her friend tossed her golden curls. "You should not have given him the opportunity. Now he'll think you're sweet on him."

Emily wrinkled her nose. "I rather doubt that. As soon as I realized what was happening, I jumped up as if he were on fire. Why would he do something like that, Pris? Hug me, I mean."

"A scoundrel like Lord Robert prides himself on his ability to turn a lady's head," Priscilla said, voice stern with authority. "I do not trust sweet words, Emily. They rarely lead to anything but trouble."

Emily frowned. "But what if the fellow is sincere?"

Priscilla waved a hand. "If he is sincere, he'll offer for you, preferably with a diamond of some sort in hand."

Lord Robert had offered. And she supposed he hadn't held out a diamond or any other jewel because his family was not well off. Yet he claimed everything was fine financially. Oh, was she ever to learn the truth about the fellow?

Priscilla had returned to her spot between the shutters. In the shadowed coach, the sounds of London came softly: the rattle of carriages passing, the rumble of wheels and clatter of hooves on cobblestones. But the longer they sat there, the more Emily's nerves tensed. Perhaps following Robert again wasn't such a good idea. What if he were a worse scoundrel than she thought? What if he saw Daphne and Ariadne following him?

What if he were no villain after all, and Emily caused a scandal greater than Priscilla's aunt?

"There's Berry Brothers," Priscilla commented. "Purveyors of fine wine. They have a scale big enough to weigh a man upon." She pulled back to eye Emily. "I wonder if I could prevail upon them to lend it for our guests' amusement at the ball."

Emily nodded but with no feeling. Would Lord Robert remember Daphne and Ariadne from their brief meeting at His Grace's town house? They had said the least to him.

"Oh!" Priscilla cried.

Emily stiffened. "What? Are they in danger?"

"No," she pouted, nose to the crack in the shutters. "You should see the crowds at Harris's. The new lavender water must have come in, and we're missing it!"

"Will you please attend to our task?" Emily hissed.

Priscilla waved a hand in her direction. Mr. Wells turned the horses to circle the block.

By the time they started down St. James's again, Emily's foot was tapping on the floor. What if Lord Robert suspected their purpose? Surely he wouldn't accost her friends on a public street. But what if he drew them into an alley? It was not unknown for young ladies to disappear in the dark of London. Maybe he really *was* smuggling virgins! What had she done?

"Give over," she demanded, shoving Priscilla away from the window.

"Well, I like that," Priscilla said with a sniff, throwing herself back into her seat. "May I remind you, *Lady* Emily, that this is my carriage?"

"Yes, yes," Emily said. "And this is my future." She peered through the crack. Where were Daphne and Ariadne? Where was he? Other carriages passed, blocking her view. A group of gentlemen erupted from one of the clubs, crowding the pavement with the sound of their husky laughter.

Mr. Wells slowed the carriage, then stopped it, and she caught sight of Ariadne's pink pelisse. Emily barely fell back from the door before the girl snatched it open, and she and her sister jumped in.

"He just hailed a hack," Daphne said as she fell into her seat. "Heading south, toward Pall Mall."

Priscilla rapped on the panel. "Did you hear that, Mr. Wells?"

"South toward Pall Mall. Very good, miss." He called to the horses, and the carriage picked up speed.

"Well?" Priscilla demanded as Ariadne sat fanning herself with one hand. "What happened?"

"I'm so glad you convinced me to go," Daphne answered, voice trembling in her excitement. "It was beyond delightful. He visited an apothecary, a haberdashery, and a perfumery. Lord Snedley never mentioned that men needed perfume."

"Spare me his shopping list," Emily said. "Did he do nothing interesting?"

It turned out that he had done nothing they could connect to what they already suspected about the man. But at least, with Lord Robert safely ensconced in another carriage, they could open the shutters and watch the city pass as they chased him.

He led them around the gatehouse to St. James's Palace, the redbrick towers with banners flying looking like something out of a medieval fairy tale, then on toward palatial Carlton House, where the Prince Regent lived. Grand churches with beggars on their stone steps, businesses with dark-coated gentlemen scurrying to and fro, and shops crowded with London's most fashionable flew past their windows. Watching all the grandeur, Emily nearly forgot about the chase.

It wasn't until they reached the shopping district of Fleet Street that Lord Robert stopped again, leaving his hired hack to loiter in front of a modiste's shop as fashionable as Madam Levasard's. Daphne left the shutters open just the slightest, so that they all could see. The ladies inside the dressmaker's shop noticed him as well. Emily could see them peering out the window and whispering behind their hands.

Another lady strolled up, and by the way she smiled at Lord Robert and held out her hand, Emily did not think the two of them had just happened to meet. She had black hair that cascaded down her back in heavy curls, and an emerald velvet hat with a single peacock feather waving over the flat top. Jeweled bobs dangled from her ears, and fur trimmed her jacket. A maid with a ribboned cap was standing just behind, trying to pretend she was invisible.

"That's the Marchioness of Skelcroft!" Ariadne exclaimed. "I've seen her caricature in the papers."

"And those are diamonds at her ears," Priscilla added. "And see the drape of that gown? Straight out of *La Belle Assemblée*, the ladies' fashion magazine."

As they watched, Lord Robert raised her hand to his lips and held it there far too long. Lady Skelcroft tilted her head to gaze up at him. Emily could almost hear her giggle from the carriage. She reached for her locket and held on tight.

"She's married, you know," Ariadne said quietly. "And her husband is worth five thousand pounds a year."

"That must be the married woman with whom he dallied," Emily said, amazed the words came so calmly when her heart was hitting her chest so painfully. How could he look at that woman so tenderly when only yesterday he'd held Emily in his arms? "Does it appear to you that the dalliance is ended?"

As if he knew she was watching, Lord Robert turned suddenly and walked away. The lady's smile faded. Her shoulders hunched in the fine jacket, making her look far older. She turned and barked something to her maid, who scurried after her as they continued down the street.

"Perhaps," Priscilla allowed. "Oh, boys can be so unfair!"

"I think she's the one who's unfair," Daphne said, raising her chin. "She should have been loyal to her husband. Lord Snedley would have insisted upon it."

"Well, it looks as if her husband is stingy," Priscilla said, as if that excused the lady's actions. "I've seen a set of ear bobs very like those. Aunt Sylvia had them. *Her* husband bought her a matching brooch."

Emily narrowed her eyes. "Perhaps Lady Skelcroft had a matching brooch as well, before she met Lord Robert."

"Oh," Ariadne said with a delighted shiver. "Yes, of course. What if he stole something from every lady with whom he dallied? I can see the headline now: 'He could not steal their hearts, so he stole their jewels instead!'" She reached for her reticule and started hunting for her journal.

"But we've already established that he could not have stolen Acantha's pearls," Priscilla pointed out. "She merely misplaced them."

"Perhaps he didn't steal from Acantha," Daphne said. "Even jewel thieves must have some standards."

"At least you know he isn't after your jewels, Emily," Ariadne said, obviously unwilling to give up the idea. "He actually offered for you."

That was small consolation. Besides, if he'd stolen jewels from all the ladies with whom he'd dallied, why weren't any of them complaining? Emily could not understand him. Was he or *wasn't* he a scoundrel?

From Fleet Street Robert hailed a hack to Doctors' Commons. So close to the Thames, the air was thick with the briny tang of the river. The heavy stone buildings sat around a center courtyard, and Emily and the others could see men and women of all walks of life hurrying back and forth. Close at hand, a family stood with heads bowed, faces pinched, their black coats and hats proclaiming them to be in mourning.

"That building is where wills are debated," Ariadne explained.

Across the way, three gentlemen strode out of another building. Seeing Lord Robert, they paused to clap him on the back and offer their hands. Emily was at a loss as to why.

Ariadne looked at her with pity. "That's the only place in England you can purchase a Special License to marry."

Emily felt ill.

She felt no better as the afternoon wore on. The sun was setting as Lord Robert returned to his club. Daphne and Ariadne were nodding off in their seats, and Mr. Wells reminded Priscilla that the horses needed their beds.

"He must have seen us," Priscilla said as they watched the lamplighter approach on St. James's. "That is the only explanation for his exemplary behavior today."

Emily shook her head. This was maddening! She couldn't go another night wondering whether Lord Robert was true in his courtship, worrying that she would never see the ball. She had to discover his secret, to save her future and her sanity.

"Wait," Priscilla said from the window. "I think he's just come out again, on foot." She turned to Emily. "Shall I have Mr. Wells follow him?"

"No," Emily said, opening her evening cloak and slipping it about her shoulders. "If he's on foot, I shall follow him this time."

"Oh, Lady Emily," Daphne cried, "you can't! Think of your reputation if you are caught!"

"Better a tarnished reputation than a life married to Lord

Robert," Emily countered, though her heart began beating more quickly at the thought.

"At least with a tarnished reputation you'll be less attractive to the slave markets," Ariadne said, as if that would cheer her.

"Just keep me in sight," Emily told them.

They nodded, wide-eyed, and she climbed from the carriage.

Mr. Wells looked startled to see her, but no more startled than she to see the changes in St. James's with the twilight. Gone were the strolling dandies, the fashionable ladies. The women across the street were no ladies at all, their lips bloodred as the lamplight flared to life above them.

Shadows leapt away from her, growing larger. Emily felt as if unseen fingers reached out to drag her down. Even the air seemed colder as she sucked in a breath. She would never dare show her face in the daylight again if it were known she'd been so foolhardy as to venture down St. James's after dark.

But she would not give up. Before Mr. Wells could stop her, Emily pulled her hood about her head and hurried off.

Lord Robert was heading away from White's into the area where the lamplighter had yet to go, leading her deeper into the darkness. Emily's hands clutched the cloak about her, clammy. In the dusk, she could just make out the chestnut of Robert's hair. What had he done with his hat? There was also something odd about the way he moved, hunched over, shuffling along as if daring her to follow. Did he know she was there, or had he already had too much wine? Did she truly want to face him when he was foxed?

Suddenly, he darted into an alley. Was he at last involving himself in scandal? Emily glanced back to make sure the carriage was following, then crept to the corner and peered around it.

A large hand reached out and grabbed her cloak. She barely managed a gasp before she was tugged into the darkness.

·17·

To Dally in
a Dark Alley

Smells assailed Emily, rancid, cloying, and something brushed past her skirts with a cry. She wanted to cry out herself, but she couldn't seem to find her voice.

"What are you doing?" Jamie demanded.

She nearly fainted in relief as she realized who held her. "I might ask you the same question," she countered as he released her.

"I'm trying to keep you out of trouble, though you don't make it easy." He straightened, and she realized he had been the hunched figure she'd followed.

"You knew I was following Lord Robert?" she asked. "How?"

"Because I was following him," he said. In the dim light, she could see him shake his head. The space did not seem so terrifying now, with him beside her.

"I spotted your friends on St. James's Street this morning," he explained, "peering behind their hands, hiding in doorways. I saw them run to the carriage and caught a glimpse of you inside. I'm amazed Lord Robert didn't catch on. Didn't you learn anything last time? It's not safe for you out alone like this."

With a rattle of tack and the clatter of horses' hooves, Priscilla's carriage drew up opposite the entrance to the alley.

"All right there, your ladyship?" Mr. Wells called, looking as though he meant to leap off the box and come to her rescue.

"Fine, Mr. Wells," Emily called back. She waved a hand to keep him on the carriage, then lifted her head sweetly to Jamie. "You were saying?"

"If I meant to do you harm, you'd have been dead before he got here."

The air left her lungs in a rush. "Oh!"

He put a hand on her elbow as if to steady her. "Now do you see the danger?"

"Lord Robert doesn't want to kill me," she pointed out, though the night seemed colder again. "He wants to marry me."

"So would a great many other fine gentlemen, if you'd give them the chance."

She couldn't help the grin that was forming. "Thank you."

Goodness, was he blushing? It seemed to her that his skin had darkened in the twilight.

"My point was," he said, "that you don't need a blackguard like Lord Robert Townsend. A lady like you could do better."

"Lady Emily?" Now Ariadne called. "If he is in league with slavers, nod once."

Emily threw up her hands and turned. "I said I'm fine. It isn't Lord Robert; it's a friend. Give me a moment."

She could hear the amusement in his voice as she turned to him. "Slavers?"

"Pay her no heed. Suffice it to say that I would like to prove that Lord Robert is an insufferable brute as much as you apparently do."

"I always knew you were smart," he said, voice now tinged with admiration. "But I can't let you risk yourself like this."

"My dear Mr. Cropper," she said, "do you have a choice?"

He sighed. "I could tell His Grace."

He could. If he could catch him. Still, she didn't want to chance it. "I wish you wouldn't worry my father. He has enough on his mind." She fluttered her lashes as she'd seen Priscilla do, but the light was fading more quickly every minute, and she doubted he could see her. In fact, he was rapidly becoming a shadow in the night.

"Very well," he said, "but you'll have to promise me you won't follow Lord Robert like this again."

"I can't make that promise. I told you. I must learn his secret."

"You can't just cry off? Tell your father you don't fancy the fellow after all?"

"My father thinks the world of Lord Robert. My only hope is to find some evidence of wrongdoing so I can expose Lord Robert before Priscilla's ball."

"A ball?" She could hear the frown in his voice.

"Yes. Lord Robert has forbidden me to attend it."

He shook his head. "You're risking your reputation, maybe even your life, for a ball?"

She should have sent him packing, told him it was none of his affair, but she couldn't. She needed him to understand. But how could she explain to a gentleman what a come-out ball truly meant for a young lady? All boys seemed to care about were horses and carriages!

"Are you fond of horses, Mr. Cropper?" she tried.

He cocked his head as if surprised by the change in subject. "As much as the next fellow, I suppose. Though I saw one at Tattersalls last week that was the finest little filly any man might want. I wager she'd win a race or two."

Horses it was then. "My father also owns several racehorses," she told him. "I've seen their foals in the fields. They start off small, with spindly legs that barely hold them up. Trainers work with them, encourage them. And then, one day, they set foot on the track and they fly. And nothing, nothing in the world can catch them. That's a come-out ball, Mr. Cropper. This is our time to fly."

He was silent for a moment, as if choosing his words carefully. "And Lord Robert, he doesn't want you to fly?"

She shook her head. "He and my father both think it best if I simply marry and get on with my life."

"Funny how those who love us most only want to protect us, even from our own dreams. My mother is like that. She doesn't like my intended path in life. Not gentlemanly enough. It's as if she'd prefer to see me wobbling about your field rather than running in any kind of race where I might get hurt."

He sounded as if he knew how she felt, as if he'd faced the same obstacles. Emily sighed. "Is that it, do you think? They simply don't want to see us disappointed?"

"In your case, only you can say. I'm right sorry to defend Lord Robert, believe me. I just wish I knew what he was up to."

Emily frowned. "Why?"

He stiffened as if she'd caught him doing something wrong. "Why, I'm just a curious sort of fellow, that's all."

His tone was once more casual, but she could not believe that only curiosity motivated him. "Come now, sir. I've told you why my investigation is so important to me. Why are you going out of your way to follow Lord Robert?"

"I regret that has to be my secret for yet a while, your ladyship." He sounded sincerely saddened by that fact.

"Perhaps I can help you," Emily said, an idea forming. "We're having an engagement dinner tomorrow night. Why don't you join us? At the very least, you could ask a few questions of those who know him best."

"At the Townsends? I doubt I'd be welcome."

Very likely not. Lord Robert had lashed out the moment she'd mentioned Jamie's name. But if she brought the two of them together, perhaps they all might learn a few secrets.

She put a hand on his arm. "On the contrary, Mr. Cropper. You will be most welcome. I'll ask Lady Wakenoak to add your name to the guest list, and I look forward to seeing you tomorrow night."

◦18◦
Dining with the Enemy

As she prepared for the dinner party the next night, Emily felt as tense as an overwound clock ready to spring in all directions at once. True, Jamie would be there, but she had no assurance that he would do any better at bringing Lord Robert's secret to light. At the moment, she had nothing to hand His Grace, just unconnected circumstances.

And time was running out.

She'd attended services with His Grace at St. George's Hanover Square that morning and spent a few moments praying for insight. She'd also attempted to reason with His Grace again as they walked home. He was thoughtful, as he usually was, listening intently while she shared the horrors of Lady St. Gregory's recent visit. He was a diplomat after all. Encouraged by his comments, she'd even tried telling him about racehorses and balls. But in the end, he was firm.

"You've given me no logical reason to refuse Lord Robert's request," he said. "You do not need this ball to become a lady. You were born a lady. And you do not need to join the Royal Society to paint. I'm certain Lord Robert will be delighted to have an easel set up for you somewhere."

Given how kind Lord Robert had been to bring Lady St.

Gregory to visit, he likely would. But His Grace simply did not understand. She would not feel that her life had started if she did not attend Priscilla's ball. She would go from being the Duke of Emerson's daughter to being Lord Robert Townsend's wife, a faceless, graceless creature with no standing of her own. Was there no time in which she might be simply Lady Emily Southwell?

She was glad Priscilla was coming with her and His Grace tonight. Mr. Tate was busy settling his sister's affairs, and Mrs. Tate was overset with the megrims, meaning that she was too nervous to attend an event where she feared censure. Emily only wished *she* had that excuse to stay away.

Anyone else, she was sure, would be delighted with the event. The Townsends had done everything to make the night memorable. Emily, Priscilla, and His Grace were greeted at the door by a tall footman in a white powdered wig and blue-and-gold livery, who took their wraps and escorted them up the sweeping staircase to the elegant withdrawing room. Already a dozen people waited among the perfectly matched chairs, all done in blue velvet with gold trim. Grecian columns decorated the doors and window wells and a double row flanked the massive marble fireplace. Ariadne and Daphne, standing next to it in white silk gowns, looked as if they had just left the temple. Even Lady Rollings, standing with her husband to the side where she could keep an eye on things, looked pleased with them.

Of course, Emily and Priscilla were not allowed to go straight to Daphne and Ariadne's side. Instead, a lady in a fashionable rose gown and silver turban rushed forward to take His Grace's hand. "Emerson, Lady Emily," she gushed, "how very good to see you again."

Lady Wakenoak was much as Emily remembered her: round-faced, heavy-bosomed, soft-voiced, the sort of perfumed lady she'd seen staring out of old portraits all over England. The new Lord Wakenoak, Robert's brother, she would have preferred to forget. He was tall and heavy and dour-faced, as if this evening could not end quickly enough for him.

At least they had that in common.

His Grace introduced Priscilla, and then Lord Robert's mother led them around the room to meet everyone else. Emily had long ago learned to make a game of it; it was the only way to remember all the names and titles.

Countess Baminger had a big behind. Lady Eglantine had a nose like an elephant. The Marquess of Skelcroft was as skinny as a skeleton with hands nearly as cold; Emily felt them through her gloves.

She did not think it any better excuse for the Marchioness of Skelcroft to have looked Lord Robert's way. The woman was quite snippy to Emily, and Emily could not imagine what Lord Robert saw in her either. Up close, it was easy to notice that Lady Skelcroft was years older than he was, and, by the way she kept touching her long black curls, hopelessly vain.

"What were you thinking?" Priscilla demanded of Emily when they at last joined Ariadne and Daphne. "You look as if you're in mourning!"

"I feel as if I'm in mourning," Emily replied, glancing down at the somber gray gown she'd chosen. At least the matte satin had silver embroidery all along the modest neck and cap sleeves, and her long gloves and slippers were of the same material.

"I think she looks perfect," Ariadne said. "The despondent heroine, still struggling for her freedom."

Priscilla shook her head. Of course, no one would find her less than perfect. Only the other members of La Petite Four would recognize that gown. Emily was certain it was the one her aunt Sylvia had had made for Priscilla before Easter, a lovely lavender confection of floaty silk gauze and a daringly low neckline. More than one gentleman had raised his quizzing glass as if to get a better look at her as she had passed.

"So?" Daphne prodded. "Tell us! How are we to best Lord Robert?"

"Indeed," Ariadne agreed, accepting a crystal glass of rosy liquid from a footman. She took a sniff and wrinkled her nose. "Ratafia. Why is this flowery stuff so popular? I am highly tempted to try the sherry, for research purposes, of course."

Daphne glanced at their frowning mother and shook her head. "Mother's watching."

Ariadne sighed. "When is Mother not watching? She has a thousand rules, and I've heard each one at least twice!" She turned to Emily. "When do you expect Mr. Cropper?"

Emily's stomach tightened. "Any moment. Lady Wakenoak very graciously agreed to invite him, even though asking her so late was a terrible breach in etiquette."

"Lord Snedley would be appalled," Daphne agreed. "But sometimes drastic measures are needed."

"And Mr. Cropper may not be drastic enough," Priscilla said, foot tapping. "I doubt you will fend Lord Robert off so easily, Emily. He seems determined to make certain London knows he is marrying you. Everyone here is well connected in Society. They will be merciless if you jilt him for the ball."

Now Emily's throat tightened as well, quite as if someone had set a noose about her neck and squeezed. Before she could answer, however, the footman appeared in the doorway.

"Lord Robert Townsend, Lord Benjamin Quincy, and the Honorable Mr. Horatio Cunningham," he announced.

Emily could hear the intake of breath. Really, Priscilla, Daphne, and Ariadne had no control around the gentlemen. Yet, even knowing Lord Robert was likely a scoundrel, she could not take her eyes off him and his friends as they made their way around the room.

The three were like young gods strolling about: tall, broad-shouldered, and long-limbed, all dressed in dark coats and white satin knee breeches. One of Lord Robert's friends had hair as golden as Priscilla's, that curled lazily over his brow. The other had hair as black as ebony, short-cropped, and as dramatic as his angular features.

Hercules, Apollo, and Hades. Only La Petite Four knew Lord Robert very likely deserved the title of Lord of the Underworld more than his dark-haired friend. Even Lady Rollings looked impressed when he bowed over her hand. He had a smile for every kind word, a self-deprecating jest for every bit of praise.

"Did you see that?" Priscilla whispered. "Lady Skelcroft simpered at Lord Robert. She is *clearly* still enamored of him."

"Perhaps," Emily allowed, "though I doubt I could hold down my ratafia if she simpered at me."

Beside her, she felt Ariadne begin to shake. Glancing at her friend, Emily saw that Ariadne's gaze had dropped to the toes of her white satin evening slippers, and her skin was so pale, it was nearly translucent.

"Ariadne?" she asked with a frown. "What is it?"

"Shush!" Ariadne begged. "Here they come. Oh, I never know what to say to gentlemen!"

"It's only Lord Robert's friends, silly," Daphne said, taking a step closer, as if to comfort her. "They're very likely no better than he is."

"Nonsense," Ariadne said heatedly, raising her gaze long enough to glare at her sister. "Just because Lord Robert is horrid, it need not follow that he must have horrid friends. They might have been blinded by his charm, just like poor Lavinia Haversham."

There was no more time for encouragement, for the gentlemen were upon them. Lord Robert took Emily's free hand and clasped it in both of his.

"Forgive me for not rushing to your side, my darling," he begged. "Duty, you know."

Emily kept her look cool as she retrieved her hand. "Pray allow me to do mine, then. You remember my dear friends Miss Priscilla Tate, Misses Daphne and Ariadne Courdebas."

They all dipped curtsies, and Emily was only thankful that Ariadne did not wobble. She still looked as if she might faint as Lord Robert's friends gazed at her.

"Ladies," Lord Robert said with a nod. "How wonderful you could join us tonight. I must make my friends known to you. Viscount Quincy and Mr. Cunningham pride themselves on knowing every beautiful young lady in London."

There he went calling them beautiful again. Truly, he used the word at the least provocation. Still, Ariadne swayed, and Daphne swallowed as if to keep herself from drooling.

"Charmed," Lord Quincy drawled, making him sound anything but. Perhaps he deserved the title of Hades after all.

"Enchanted," Mr. Cunningham said with a gamin grin. "And may I say you look lovely tonight, Miss Courdebas and Miss Courdebas. There is nothing like a lady gowned in purest white."

"I told you so," Daphne hissed with a swift elbow in Ariadne's side.

That was all it took. Ariadne's hands were shaking so much that the bump broke her hold on the glass's stem. She stared in obvious horror as the goblet tumbled to the Oriental carpet, splashing her rosy beverage all down the front of her gown.

"Or red, it seems," Viscount Quincy drawled.

Ariadne's face was scarlet. "Excuse me, please," she muttered before fleeing the room.

Emily did not wait to see what Lord Robert or his friends would do and hurried after Ariadne. Priscilla might consider the matter before deciding that the company of three handsome gentlemen was much to be preferred, even if one *was* an unconscionable scoundrel. Daphne would no doubt be too busy trying to remember Lord Snedley's advice for removing stains from silk. Ariadne needed help *now*.

Emily caught up with her in the corridor just outside the withdrawing room. "Are you all right?" she asked.

Ariadne sniffled, the candlelight from the golden sconce on the wall casting delicate shadows on her tearstained face. "Oh, I shall survive."

"At least you won't have to wear that dress again," Emily pointed out. "Knowing how you feel about white, I imagine that will be a relief."

Ariadne giggled through her tears. "There is that. Oh, Emily, was there ever a bigger fool?"

Emily linked her arm with Ariadne's and led her toward the door to the ladies' retiring room. "Nonsense. Anyone could spill. I'm certain there must be some remedy. What would Lord Snedley advise?"

"Something terribly useless, no doubt. But don't fret over me. You should go back. This evening is in your honor, after all. I'll be along shortly. Just don't let Priscilla latch onto all the Eligibles."

Emily wanted to protest. She had no wish to return to that

room, to be gaped at and talked about, to pretend that she was enjoying the prospect of marrying Lord Robert. But Ariadne had a point, and Emily knew she shouldn't stay away from the festivities for long.

So she turned, squared her shoulders, and told herself she could do this. She *had* to do this. Too much was at stake.

Then she saw him.

Jamie stood in the corridor for a moment before turning and murmuring something to the footman just behind, as if he preferred to enter the room unannounced. Emily wasn't sure why. He certainly looked the part of a gentleman: black coat, black breaches buckled at his knees, a green-striped waistcoat, and a simply tied but absolutely spotless cravat. His hands were encased in white kid gloves, and his evening shoes were every bit as shiny as Lord Robert's.

Seeing her there, he touched two fingers to his forehead. "Mr. James Cropper, reporting as requested, your ladyship."

Hope rushed through her. Here was an ally, a helper Lord Robert and his friends could not intimidate. Yet as she walked toward him, she noticed that his smile was not quite as bright as she remembered, as if he was unsure of his welcome, unsure of her. She saw questions were written in those gray eyes, questions she wasn't sure how to answer.

Lady Skelcroft and Lady Baminger exited the withdrawing room just then and stopped when they saw Jamie standing there. Lady Baminger merely frowned, but Lady Skelcroft's mouth opened and closed as her face paled. Then she hurried past Emily for the retiring room.

"Do you know her?" Emily could not help asking Jamie.

He opened his mouth to answer, but Lord Robert strolled out of the withdrawing room, every bit as if he had been following the ladies. He too jerked to a stop at the sight of Jamie, his handsome face flushing red.

"What are you doing here?" he demanded.

❖ 19 ❖
The Rules of Engagement

Jamie stared at Lord Robert, and Lord Robert stared back. This was what Emily had planned, but she felt as stretched and taut as one of her canvases. What if they came to blows? Lord Robert might lose his handsome face to Jamie's knuckles, but she was more concerned for Jamie. Striking an aristocrat was a hanging offense for a commoner.

She dashed up to them and placed herself squarely between them. "*I* invited Mr. Cropper, Lord Robert. It seemed as if the two of you had much to discuss."

Lord Robert grabbed Emily's arm and linked it through his own. "Mr. Cropper," he said, spitting out the name as if he'd eaten a bug, "and I have nothing to say to each other. He should have refused your invitation."

"I dislike refusing a lady," Jamie grit out with equal venom.

Beyond them, Emily saw Ariadne scamper out of the ladies' retiring room. Her face was flushed, and the ribbon around her waist was askew. Meeting Emily's gaze, she started forward, only to jerk to a stop when she saw Mr. Cropper and Lord Robert.

"The lady is unaware of the implications," Lord Robert sneered to Jamie. "You, however, are not. If you had any notion of good breeding, you would have refused."

Had Emily truly put Jamie in such a difficult position? Obviously he knew how to get along in Good Society. Why would good breeding demand that he stay away?

And what was wrong with Ariadne? Her friend stood down the corridor, mouthing words at her. It looked a bit like "He's a dastard."

Yes, Lord Robert certainly was! Emily just wished she could prove it.

"You'd definitely be more familiar with good breeding than I am," Jamie said. "You have all the trappings—fine house, fine clothes, paste jewels."

Emily tugged her arm from Lord Robert's grip. He was obviously too focused on Jamie to notice. "Starting rumors, are you, Cropper?" he demanded.

"Or investigating one."

Investigating paste jewels? Why? The girls had already established that Lord Robert *wasn't* a jewel thief, much to Emily's dismay.

Ariadne was still trying to get her attention. Now she seemed to be saying, "He's his mother."

But that made even less sense! *"What?"* Emily mouthed back.

Lord Robert leaned closer to Jamie, eyes narrowing. "I'll not have you questioning my guests. This is my home, and you cannot accuse me without a writ from the magistrate."

Accuse him? Of what? Had her suspicions been correct after all?

"Now why would I accuse you, my lord?" Jamie asked, meeting his gaze without flinching. "You being such an upstanding gentleman and all."

Lord Robert drew himself up. "It is because I am a gentleman, Mr. Cropper, that I don't have the footman throw you out on your ear. You are a guest in my home, and I know how to treat guests, just like my father."

Jamie blanched.

Emily grabbed her skirts with both hands to keep from reaching out to him. This wasn't about stolen jewels or smuggled virgins. The injury was deep, on both sides. The pain radiated like heat from a wildfire. She wanted to soothe the wound, but she had no idea what had caused it.

"Does this have anything to do with Lavinia Haversham?" she ventured.

Lord Robert jerked away from her. "Enough! Do you see the damage you've done by insinuating yourself into my fiancée's life, Cropper? If anything happens to her, I'll blame you!"

"Emily?"

Relief fell like cool rain at the sound of His Grace's voice. Here was someone who knew how to navigate difficult situations. That calm determination had settled disputes between squabbling monarchs and warring nations. She let go of her skirts and grabbed the arm of her father's coat, pulling him into the corridor.

"Father," she said with a smile. "May I present to you Mr.

James Cropper, an acquaintance of Lord Robert's and mine?"

For the barest of moments, her father hesitated, staring at Jamie, and Emily found herself staring at her father, her arms falling to her sides. Why didn't he move? Her father was never at a loss for words, never discomposed. Could His Grace know Lord Robert's secret?

Then His Grace held out his hand with a smile. "Mr. Cropper, a pleasure to meet you, sir. Please give my regards to your mother and assure her that she is remembered kindly."

Now Lord Robert was staring as well, sweat beading on his brow, but Jamie's smile reappeared.

"Thank you, Your Grace," he said, shaking hands. "Mother speaks highly of you as well."

Had Emily somehow drifted out to sea? She'd lost all landmarks, had no northern star to guide her. His Grace knew James Cropper's mother?

But how? Emily herself hadn't even seen her father in months!

"Forgive me for interrupting your conversation," His Grace continued smoothly, as if he did not notice her standing there with her mouth open, "but I believe Lord Wakenoak is awaiting us in the library."

The library. The settlement papers. Something as thick as oil paint squirmed in her stomach. She could not make herself move as her father offered his arm.

He frowned. "Emily? Did you hear me?"

She did, to her everlasting regret. The dread in her stomach solidified into a rock. How she wished she could turn away— scrape Lord Robert off her life as she scraped away an unwanted blob of paint.

There had to be something she could do!

"Yes, Father," she said, placing her arm on his. "I heard you."

Her father smiled, then nodded farewell to Mr. Cropper. She could feel Jamie's gaze on her as she passed. What would she see if she dared to meet his gaze? Sympathy? Pity?

She couldn't look.

Lord Robert fell into step behind them as they made their way down the corridor, like an executioner carrying the ax to the block.

She tightened her grip on her father's arm, forcing him to pause. "Must we do this, Father?" she whispered. "I . . . I'm not feeling well."

He patted her hand, gaze warm and soft. "There, now. These are only bridal jitters. It is my duty not to let you fall prey to them and pass up so excellent a match."

Her face felt like a mask, stiff and hot. "But the ball."

"I assure you, Emily," Lord Robert said, coming up beside them, his gaze just as warm, "there will be others."

No, there wouldn't. Not like this one. Who but Priscilla and the prince would have goldfish?

"There, you see?" His Grace said, squeezing her hand. "You have no reason for concern. I am persuaded that Lord Robert will make you a wonderful husband. And I only want the best for you.

You understand that, don't you?"

Emily managed a nod. She knew His Grace had her interests at heart. She simply had to find something to convince him her interests lay elsewhere. But she was out of ideas.

As they started forward again, the weight in her stomach grew heavier, spreading through her legs down to her feet. By the time they reached the library at the end of the corridor, she felt as though she'd walked ten miles. It seemed to take another ten to reach the desk before the fire, where Lord Wakenoak stood with a short man wearing spectacles, a solicitor.

"I've already signed," Lord Robert's brother announced as they gathered around him. "As the head of the family, I agree to the allowance being granted to my brother."

Allowance. Emily supposed she should care how much income Lord Robert brought to the marriage. She'd never thought to ask. His Grace did not seem at all concerned as he stepped forward to sign.

"And there's my agreement," he said, handing the quill back to the solicitor. "A fine dowry for my lovely daughter, with plenty of pin money to keep her in the finest of gowns."

As if she cared about gowns. She'd prefer to spend the money on paints. Perhaps she could muddle along without the Royal Society's acceptance. She might hire a tutor, someone with more experience. Perhaps she could find the time to study between managing a household and producing an heir . . .

Her stomach shoved the weight up against her chest. *An heir.*

Oh, Lord. She could not imagine being intimate with Lord Robert. She had a hard time thinking about being intimate with anyone. The rock squeezed against her lungs, making it almost impossible to gasp in a breath.

The solicitor dipped the feather pen in the crystal ink bottle and lifted the quill. Emily watched as the black drops fell from the sharp white point. The man held it out to her. Her fingers felt too heavy to take it.

"And now you, Lady Emily," he prompted as if she could not guess why he'd offered her a pen. "Your signature indicates your willingness to give the estate you inherited from your mother to Lord Robert. As your husband, he will control all your worldly goods while he lives."

He would control everything she was and everything she did. How could she agree to that?! Emily didn't want the pen, didn't want to sign, and certainly didn't want to give Lord Robert her mother's estate or her heart. She wanted to shout at all of them to go away and leave her alone. She reached for her locket and realized she'd left it at home.

She managed to squeeze an ounce of air into her lungs. They had logic and family alignments on their side. All she had were feelings—frail, unreliable feelings—to offer in protest. Feelings would do her no good this day.

She reached out, gripped the quill pen, bent, and signed her name. It was probably for the last time. Very soon she'd be Lady Emily Townsend. She had lost her future and herself.

Lord Robert took the pen from her with a smile that seemed far too big and bright for the dark room and finished his signature with a flourish.

"Well done," his brother said. "This was Father's dream, to unite our families. Let us share the good news with our guests."

His Grace moved with Lord Wakenoak toward the door, leaving the solicitor to sand the documents and pack them away. Lord Robert took Emily's arm.

"Feeling better now?" he asked as he led her toward the door.

Emily took a deep breath at last. "No, not really. I wasn't ready for this, Robert."

"Oh, you seem ready enough," he said cheerfully as they started down the corridor once more. "You've been quite busy, following me around, listening to lies, spreading your own."

The corridor seemed to tilt around her. She could not have heard him right. "I beg your pardon?"

"Your apology is a start. I expect better behavior from you from here on out. You will keep your mouth shut, around my friends and yours. You will not cavort with trash like James Cropper. That includes a tart like Priscilla Tate and nonentities like the Courdebas sisters."

The pressure was crawling up her throat, threatening to choke her. "Is this your idea of a joke?" she tried.

"Not in the slightest," he said, pausing in the doorway to the withdrawing room, where the guests stood with champagne in their hands. "As your husband, I expect you to do exactly as I say.

It will go poorly for you if you don't. And I will hear no more nonsense about you painting either. I thought you would take the hint when I brought Lady St. Gregory to visit. Having a wife who fancies herself an artist is entirely too embarrassing, particularly when she's of no real talent."

He strolled into the room, and Emily stumbled after him, the cheers of congratulations ringing in her ears.

"Wish us happy, everyone!" Lord Robert called. "Lady Emily will be my bride by this Thursday."

Lady Emily would be dead by Wednesday. She could not live with this pain, this bleak future. The room was darkening. Her senses coalesced into a burning pain in her throat. She'd just signed her life over to a monster.

"To the happy couple," Mr. Cunningham called, raising his glass. "May their union be long and prosperous."

Silk and satin rustled as everyone's arms were raised in toast.

Everyone's but Jamie's.

Emily's gaze met Jamie's, and the sounds around her faded, the people vanished, until Jamie was everything. He stood there so stiffly, as if he were in pain. Gone was his wicked smile. His remarkably fine gray eyes were dark, accusatory.

He didn't understand how she could agree to marry a scoundrel like Lord Robert. She didn't understand either, especially when she realized she could never love Lord Robert.

She loved Jamie.

Jamie challenged her, but only when she was being less than

her best. He protected her, even when she would have preferred to do so herself. He cherished her, consistently putting her needs before his own. He made it clear he valued her thoughts and opinions. He saw Emily for herself, good and bad.

And he liked her for who she was, even if she was the daughter of a duke.

She wanted to call out to him, fly to his side, take his hand, and pull him from the room. As if he could read her mind, Jamie set down his glass without taking a sip and started toward her.

Emily raised her head, begging him with her eyes to understand, to say something, to do something. Lord Robert stood smiling triumphantly, accepting the praises being thrown their way. He didn't seem to notice as Jamie drew to Emily's side.

"Is this what you wanted, then?" Jamie asked, jaw tight. "I thought you invited me here to learn enough to stop him. I thought we had the same goal. Apparently I was mistaken. Goodbye, Lady Emily."

He brushed past her, leaving the room, leaving the house, leaving her life.

The darkness inside Emily spilled into her mouth, burning, suffocating. She couldn't bear the sight of all these smiling people, couldn't bear to hear another word in congratulations, couldn't breathe.

She only found her breath again after she was sick, all over Lord Robert's shiny black evening shoes.

✦20✦
Shattered Dreams

His Grace was solicitous as he tucked the ermine lap robe around Emily in the coach after they'd abruptly left the Townsends. "There, now. I'm sure it was simply too much excitement this evening. You'll feel better in the morning."

Emily sincerely doubted that. She would never have an opportunity to prove herself to Society. Her art would soon be a thing of the past. She was set to marry a vile villain. And, worst of all, the man she loved thought her faithless. She thought she might never feel well again.

Priscilla, Daphne, and Ariadne had been just as concerned, clustering around her for only a moment before His Grace had whisked her away. Ariadne's face was long and mournful, and her lips trembled as if she struggled with what to say. Priscilla looked worse, her color gone, one arm wrapped around the lavender gauze as she hugged herself. Daphne took Emily in her arms and held her close, as if trying to be strong for them both. For a moment, all Emily could do was stand and soak up the warmth.

"This is a terrible injustice," Ariadne murmured, laying a hand on Emily's shoulder. "But we will prevail."

How, Emily could not see.

"I hate to question you when you're feeling poorly," her father continued now, leaning back against the blue cushions as the carriage started for home. "But you mentioned that you were acquainted with Mr. Cropper. How did you meet him?"

Where to start? She'd been seeing him around London for the last week and at Barnsley before that. Of course, had she realized it, she'd been dreaming of him her whole life—a man who would appreciate her art, appreciate her. A man she could trust with her heart.

"He came to the house to see you a few days ago," she said. "Warburton said he had a letter of introduction."

Her father frowned. "He did not approach me."

Because he'd known her father already favored Lord Robert. She frowned. But why would that make a difference? What had Lord Robert to do with her father and Jamie?

"I believe," Emily said carefully, "that he is following Lord Robert."

"Unlikely," her father replied. "I can think of no reason for Bow Street to be interested in the Townsends."

Bow Street? Of course! Jamie must be a Runner, part of London's elite investigative force. He had to be one of the youngest, but by no means the least talented, she was sure. That's what he'd meant when he said his mother would have preferred him to have another vocation. That's why he hadn't been able to tell her why he was following Lord Robert! And why he'd never truly been following her.

It also explained why he was so angry when he thought Emily

had prevented him from learning the truth. She would never forget the look on his face, a heartbreaking mix of pain and pride. She shivered just remembering it. He'd been investigating Lord Robert for something serious. But what?

"How do you know Mr. Cropper?" she asked her father. "You said you knew his mother."

Her father sighed. "It is not a topic I would choose to discuss with you, but as you are acquainted with the young man and about to marry Lord Robert, I suppose you had better know the truth. James Cropper is the son of the previous Lord Wakenoak, Lord Robert's father."

Emily threw off the lap robe to lean closer. That's what Ariadne had been trying to say! James Cropper is a bastard. He was Lord Robert's brother! She'd seen the resemblance from the first in that magnificent mane of hair, but she found she could not believe Lord Robert and Jamie to be related. "You knew Lord Wakenoak had an illegitimate child and you never told me?"

They drove near a lamp post then, and she could see His Grace looking intently at her, his brown eyes dark and grim. "There are a great many things I do not tell you, Emily Rose," he said. "Be glad for that fact."

She felt herself blushing. "Yes, well, it seems I needed to know this one."

"Indeed. It is not a happy tale. Wakenoak had his wilder moments, which I could not like. Jasmine Cropper was a delightful young woman, one of Lady Wakenoak's goddaughters come to join them for the Season." He sighed again. "It is a sad fact, Emily, that some gentlemen must have their own way, even when it hurts others."

Lord Robert came to mind. She'd always thought he was his father's favorite. It seemed they had a great deal in common, even bullying women.

"There would have been a great scandal, of course," her father said, "but Miss Cropper chose to sequester herself in a quiet corner of London and add a 'Mrs.' to her name. When I learned James had been born, I advised Wakenoak to give him every advantage. I thought he'd at least paid for tutoring, but it appears the boy had to pull himself up by his bootstraps. I'll speak to my steward. Perhaps we can find a place for him on one of the estates."

An estate manager would have been no better consort for the daughter of a duke, but she supposed it hardly mattered now. Nothing mattered now. Unless Jamie accused Lord Robert of some crime in the next two days, she was as good as married.

And even if the impossible were to happen, she had no hope of regaining Jamie's good regard. He was right. She had used him, brought him to the dinner in a desperate attempt to show up Lord Robert. He would see Emily as no better than his own father, using others for personal gain. He'd never forgive her.

She was so despondent that she had only a vague memory of entering the town house and bidding her father good night. She allowed Mary to help her change, answering questions about the big night so tersely that Mary soon gave up. But after Mary left

Emily couldn't bear the quiet of her silk-paneled room.

She went to her easel and stared at the soldiers, the roses of their badges stark red and white in the candlelight. Who cared about battles from long ago when people's hearts were breaking and dreams were shattering right here, right now? Surely there was something more important she could paint.

She hefted the larger canvas down and replaced it with the second, smaller one Miss Alexander had sent with her. She gazed at the blank canvas for the longest time, until she began to see shades of gray and blue and yellow in the expanse of cream. But nothing grand enough or beautiful enough came to mind. She simply could not paint a bowl of fruit. She'd give up painting first!

She was nearly ready to give up now. How was it Lady St. Gregory thought Emily incapable of putting herself into her battle scenes? Even Jamie had said Emily had missed the emotion. They were both wrong.

She put herself into her paintings. The bold colors made her feel stronger. The solidity of the oils gave her a sense of control, as if the world could be just as she ordered it, given time and patience. And the battle scenes, well, they were big, powerful. In them, men were heroes, and heroes triumphed. And, in a small way, so did she. Painting anything else felt limited, insignificant.

Vulnerable.

Emily turned to her paints. Her hands shook as she mixed the oils, prepared her palette. She didn't sketch the piece in charcoal first as was her usual process. She attacked the canvas, stroking on the paint surely. If no one knew what she was made of, she'd simply have to show them.

The painting blossomed under her brush. Indeed, the ease of it surprised her. Color and form blended, became real. Then love and hope and dreams mixed, slowing her hand. It was as if she painted with her own tears, her own blood.

Memory fueled each stroke—the thought of Priscilla's delighted smile, the sound of Ariadne's infectious giggle, Daphne's quiet strength. She thought of His Grace tucking the lap robe around her with care, Jamie facing down a beggar twice his size to protect her. There was warmth and bittersweet pain in remembering how many people loved her, how many people she loved.

Even if they were no longer at her side.

She stepped back finally and eyed the piece. It might never win Miss Alexander's praise or the Barnsley Prize in Art. Very likely it would never earn her Lady St. Gregory's approval or a place in the Royal Society for the Beaux Arts. But she needed no one to tell her it was very, very good.

She only wished she could say that about the rest of her life.

·21·

White Flags
of Surrender

Emily bent over Medallion's head, gloved hands on her horse's reins. "I need you to fly today," she whispered into the black ear. Medallion shook her head, the silky mane caressing Emily's cheek. She touched her heels to the horse's flank and felt the muscles bunch beneath her. In a breath, they were away.

The Thoroughbred pounded down the sandy track, the beat of her hooves echoing the pounding of Emily's heart. The air, heady with the blooms of spring, swept past her, cooling her skin, wiping clean her mind, imbuing hope, purpose.

She had two days to catch Lord Robert before the ball. She had to think, plan, determine some way to expose him to all of London.

But expose him as what? And how?

They reached the end of Rotten Row, with Kensington Palace looming in the background, and Emily pulled the horse up. Rubbing her hand along Medallion's glossy neck, she turned the horse for the walk back up Hyde Park.

And heard her name being called.

"Emily!" Daphne shouted, waving wildly from the seat of her father's barouche. Beside her in the open carriage sat Ariadne, with Priscilla on the opposite seat. They were all bundled in quilted pelisses, testimony to the morning chill. But the fact that none of them wore bonnets was testimony to the speed at which they'd come to find her.

As their family coachman reined the matching black horses to a halt, Emily brought Medallion alongside.

"We have so much to tell you!" Ariadne exclaimed.

Emily's groom, who had been following at a distance, rode up as well. Emily tossed him Medallion's reins and slid to the ground, pausing to tuck the black train of her wool riding habit up over her arm. In a moment, she had dispatched the groom to return the horse to the stable and climbed into the carriage to seat herself beside Priscilla.

"A great deal happened after you left last night," Daphne said, leaning forward as the carriage set out once more.

"A great deal happened *before* she left," Ariadne argued. She turned to Emily. "I'm only sorry I could not reach you in time. James Cropper is Lord Robert's half brother and a Bow Street Runner!"

Though merely hearing Jamie's name was painful, Emily managed a smile. "I know. Father told me on the way home."

Ariadne's face fell. "Oh, well, then."

"There is more," Daphne said, looking first at Emily and then more pointedly at Ariadne.

"Oh, I suppose," Ariadne said. "But Emily quite stole my thunder."

"Perhaps you should start at the beginning," Emily said.

Ariadne sighed, her gaze going to the trees in the copse they were crossing. "Very well. As you know, I went to the retiring room to try to fix the stain on my dress." She glanced back at Emily. "It didn't come out, by the way. You were quite right. For all my scrubbing, all I managed to do was turn the dress pink, and I know how you feel about pink."

Daphne coughed.

"I'm getting there!" Ariadne snapped. "I am a writer, you know. I can tell a decent story."

When Daphne blushed, Ariadne hurried on. "In any event, I had just stepped behind the screen to use the Necessary when who should walk in but Lady Skelcroft and Lady Baminger. That odious Lady Skelcroft was quite incensed. She was trying to decide whether to tell poor Lady Wakenoak they were dining with her husband's illegitimate son."

So Lord Robert's mother hadn't known. "I wondered why she agreed to invite him," Emily said. "I suppose I should be glad I wasn't the only one in ignorance."

"Indeed not," Ariadne assured her as the carriage passed the still, green waters of the Serpentine. "I gather Lady Baminger was just as shocked to hear. Poor Lady Wakenoak turned white when Lady Skelcroft told her after the ladies had left the gentlemen to their port and retired to the withdrawing room."

"But never you fear," Daphne put in. "Lady Skelcroft got her due. I heard her telling Lady Baminger how she'd lost her diamond brooch. Her husband feared it stolen and called Bow Street. That's how she knew Mr. Cropper."

Priscilla made a face and spoke for the first time. "You missed the end of that story when your mother called you to play the piano for everyone. Lady Skelcroft found the brooch just the other day."

Emily frowned. "Odd. That's the same thing that happened to Acantha Dalrymple."

"Well, they are just as horrid," Daphne pointed out, "and they both love calling attention to themselves so I'm not entirely surprised."

As the horses' hooves drummed against the wood bridge near Hyde Park Corner, Priscilla put a hand on Emily's arm. "I also must apologize for not speaking last night, Emily."

The ache in her voice pierced Emily's pain. She turned her frown on Priscilla. "What are you talking about?"

Priscilla's hands fluttered before her, reminding Emily of Mrs. Tate's fretting. "I wanted to tell you to fight, to refuse to marry the fellow just because your father wishes it. But I couldn't very well say that, could I? I'm guilty of the same sin."

Daphne reached out and patted Priscilla's knee. "You're only trying to help your family," she assured Priscilla.

Priscilla straightened away from the kind touch as if she did not believe she deserved it. "That may be the case for me, but it isn't the case for Emily. His Grace isn't teetering on the brink of financial disaster, and she doesn't have a Dreaded Family Secret to guard." Her green gaze sought Emily's, imploring. "You don't have to do this. Say *no*."

Emily shook her head. "It's too late, Pris. I signed the settlement papers last night. I gave my word."

Priscilla's eyes were brimming. "Only because you didn't wish to disappoint your father. You know that's the truth. You don't love Lord Robert. You couldn't love someone like him."

Tears heated Emily's eyes as well. "What was it you said, Pris? 'I imagine love and compatibility are very nice for those who can afford them.' Apparently, even a duke's daughter cannot afford them!"

"Nonsense!" Priscilla declared, dashing away her tears with one hand. "We'll go back to your town house and send the footman for Lord Robert. I very much doubt he's any match for La Petite Four when we set our minds to it. We'll tell him that enough is enough. And we'll make him give you the ball!"

Emily eyed her. Priscilla's lips were tight, her skin pale. She had no way of knowing that having the ball would not save Emily from marrying a monster or ease Emily's broken heart.

But Emily could not bear to see her friend so upset. If giving Lord Robert a piece of her mind would ease Priscilla's pain, Emily was all for it.

"I suppose it's worth a try," she agreed.

And it was far easier than she'd thought, for when they arrived at the town house, Warburton announced that Lord Robert was waiting in the withdrawing room for a word with Lady Emily.

Emily and Priscilla exchanged glances, Ariadne nodded as if she'd expected the villain to show himself, and Daphne squared her shoulders as if ready for a fight. As soon as Warburton had taken their pelisses, the girls marched into the sitting room to confront Lord Robert. Emily was surprised to find herself almost eager for the moment. Arguing with him probably wouldn't make her life any easier, as he'd no doubt take it out on her later. But she had a feeling Priscilla wouldn't be the only one relieved to lay into him.

Lord Robert rose from where he'd been sitting on the sofa. As if he saw their intent written on their determined faces, he immediately held up his hands. Surrender? It couldn't be. Emily hadn't even opened her mouth!

"Ladies, how delightful to find you all together," he said as Priscilla, Daphne, and Ariadne fanned out beside Emily, their gowns bright against the dark wool of her riding habit.

Emily crossed her arms over her chest. "Oh, really, my lord? I cannot credit that you had something you wished to say to all of us."

He must have grown used to her forthright speech, for he merely smiled as he lowered his hands. "Actually, I wished to speak to you, my dear, but I had hoped our discussion would end with an announcement of interest to your friends."

Priscilla stepped closer to Emily with a frown. "And what would that be, my lord?" Priscilla demanded.

Emily eyed her, fighting a grin. She'd never heard Priscilla take precisely that tone with a gentleman before. In fact, Priscilla sounded a great deal like Emily!

"I regret that I am not at liberty to say, Miss Tate," he replied with a short bow. "If I could have a moment of your time, Emily?"

Emily exchanged glances with Priscilla again. "Watch out for sweet words," Priscilla whispered in warning, then she stepped back and drew Daphne and Ariadne toward the door.

"We'll be just in the corridor, Lady Emily," Daphne assured her as Priscilla pulled her out. "Well within calling distance if you need us. And I know where you keep the fireplace poker." She narrowed her eyes and glared at Lord Robert before disappearing around the door frame. Ariadne, white-faced and still speechless in front of a gentleman, hurried out as well.

"Such good friends you have," Lord Robert said as Emily returned her gaze to him.

Emily raised her chin. "You did not think so last night."

"Ah," he said, clasping his hands behind his dove-colored morning coat. "And that is why I had to see you this morning. I must apologize for my behavior last night. I said some things that I regret."

Some things? She regretted every word she'd heard him speak. But Emily knew the others were listening, and she could not let La Petite Four down.

"You were a beast," she said, setting her gloved fists on her hips. "You bullied me and belittled my friends. If I were a man, I'd call you out."

His smile was all regret. "I understand how you might have

taken my words amiss. I was not myself last night. It was the sight of Cropper. The fellow has been an enemy of my family since the day he was born. To find him in our home was maddening."

She did not believe Jamie was the Townsends' enemy; he appeared to dislike Lord Robert in particular. Still, it must have shocked Lord Robert to see his half brother standing there last night. Small wonder the two had barked at each other like bull-dogs eager for a fight.

"You both said some rather harsh words," she allowed, letting her hands fall.

"I would prefer that you not dwell on that. It does me no credit. I like to think I am a gentleman."

He could pretend to the niceties all he liked. The mask had slipped last night, and Emily knew him for what he was. And he obviously thought he knew her. Did he truly find her so vapid as to believe this patter?

She tilted her head and fluttered her lashes at him. "Oh, you cannot know how that eases my mind, my lord."

He completely missed her sarcasm, smiling at Emily as if she'd performed as well as a pet pooch. "I apologize for maligning your friends as well," he said. He took a step closer, and the sunlight from the window crowned his head with fire. "I can see they have your best interests at heart. That's why I had to see you this morn-ing, before plans went any further. Perhaps I have been harsh in encouraging you to give up this ball."

A gasp rang out from the corridor, followed by a scuffling

noise, as if someone was being grabbed and hushed. Emily shook her head. She was having similar difficulty believing he meant what she thought. Surely this was some kind of trick to lull her into complacency. Why would Lord Robert give up now, when he'd won? He would think her at his mercy.

"So, you'll change your plans for me?" she asked, watching him.

"Of course," he said smoothly, as if willing to give her the world. "Though I am uncertain whether I can attend. It will all depend on Mother. Last night wore her out, poor dear, all that pretending she was happy when she is so devastated by Father's loss."

Somehow, Emily doubted Lady Wakenoak was so consummate an actress. Lord Robert's mother had seemed rather happy to have so many people about, to be dressed in finery. Which hadn't a stitch of black in it, come to think of it.

No, Lord Robert *had* to be the one acting a part. Anyone else might have been convinced by the sorrowful gaze, those down-turned lips. But she couldn't shake the feeling that he was playing some deep game, and, by agreeing to attend the ball, Emily had just dealt him the winning hand. If only he would speak the truth, just once!

She started. Of course! Last night, when he'd been in shock to see Jamie in his house, he'd spoken the truth. And Jamie had spoken the truth back. And in doing so, they had handed her the last piece of the puzzle.

She smiled up at Lord Robert so brightly, he blinked as if the sun had blinded him.

"You *must* come to the ball, my lord," she told him. "Your presence will be the highlight of the evening, I assure you."

Lord Robert smiled, obviously pleased by her insistence. He had no way of knowing that she'd just discovered his secret, and she intended to unveil it before all of London.

At the ball.

·22·

What Kind of Hermit Wanders Around Ballrooms?

Oh, but Emily had much to do before the ball! She dispatched Warburton on errands all over London, including sending an important package north by courier to her sister. Then she had to write three notes so important that her hand shook on the quill. The first was to Lady St. Gregory, telling her that there would be a painting to view after all. The second was to Lady Skelcroft, asking her to wear the diamond brooch to the ball. The lady had responded with such ill grace that Emily wished she hadn't asked.

Almost.

The third to Jamie was the hardest. She started it four times before she found a phrasing that pleased her.

Dear Mr. Cropper,
I believe there has been a misunderstanding. Please come to Miss Tate's ball tonight at nine at the Elysium Assembly Rooms near Kensington Palace, and all will be explained to your satisfaction.
Your friend, Lady Emily Southwell.

She hadn't been certain he'd answer, but the footman returned from Bow Street with the note straightaway. On the back was written in a strong, male hand, "EAR 9 L JC." The EAR, 9, and

JC she understood: He was confirming that he'd meet her at the ball at nine by including his initials. The L, however, kept her in such a dither that it was a wonder she got anything else done!

By the time she walked into the entry hall of the Elysium Assembly Rooms later that evening, Emily felt as frayed as the ends of an old shawl. She could only hope she looked better. Having had no time to get a ball gown made, she'd retrieved her mother's gown from the attic and had Mary pin her into it. Mary had also styled her hair into complicated braids and curls, with wisps escaping to tease her cheeks. The weight of the Emerson emeralds pressed down on her chest, cool, solid, impressive in their gold settings.

She would much rather have been wearing her locket. Already she missed touching it, looking at it. She would have liked that little source of comfort tonight, particularly when she alighted from the carriage on His Grace's arm. The Elysium Assembly Rooms glowed like a stone lantern in the clear spring night. Carriages crowded the drive, the rattle mixing with the sound of voices raised in excitement. The stairs to the door seemed taller, the entry hall wider. But there was Priscilla, waiting for Emily in the receiving line.

Not a fellow was going to be able to keep his eyes off her. Her delphinium blue gown was edged in white satin ruffles, with four parallel rows around the full skirt. It shimmered with light as she curtsied to her guests. The simple blue sapphire pendant around her neck called attention to the expanse of creamy white skin showing on her shoulders, and her golden curls were piled high with pearled combs to cascade down the back of her head. She was the fairy princess, presiding over her court. If she was not the toast of London by tomorrow, there was no justice in the world.

Mrs. Tate sniffed back a sob as she clutched His Grace's hand in the crowded, bustling receiving line. "So, so good of you to come," she kept warbling, as if she'd doubted that any of the 250 guests had truly meant their acceptances.

"Neither Lord Robert nor Mr. Cropper has arrived so far," Priscilla murmured to Emily as they hugged in line. "And I'm still waiting for Daphne and Ariadne."

"Then I'll wait by the door," Emily murmured back. "Did the Duke of Rottenford arrive?"

Priscilla nodded, eyes bright. "One of the first! And he actually kissed my hand!"

Oh, but the night could only get better. She hoped.

Waiting by the door, however, proved to be more difficult than Emily'd thought. She had a good view of those arriving, but an abysmal view of the ballroom itself. And where among all the silks and satins and velvets was Lord Robert?

A murmur ran through the crowd. Then people scurried out of the way as two bronzed young men, their faces perfect mirrors of each other, shouldered a sedan chair of rare ebony into the entryway. Beau Brummell stepped from the padded interior and stood for a moment, letting everyone gaze upon his glory. His nose was high, as if he resented the scent of roses on the air. He caught Emily's gaze, raised his quizzing glass to inspect her, and nodded his approval.

My word! Wait until Priscilla heard!

More cries rang out, and the Beau turned to eye the woman making her way to the front of the line. She was gowned all in gold, with jet ear bobs dangling from her lobes below her gold turban and jet beads dripping from her gown. Stalking beside her was a Scottish deerhound.

The elegant creature was immense, its black nose coming to the lady's breast bone. The dog's thick, rough, dark gray coat made it look even more powerful, and the far away look in its hazel eyes told Emily it was ready to snap its jeweled leash and run. Preferably with a stag between its sharp teeth.

"Brummell," the lady purred as she strolled past.

"Show-off," Brummell muttered.

"Did you see that?" Daphne said, hurrying to Emily's side and standing on tiptoe to catch another glimpse of the rare hound. The white gown's overskirt had been embroidered with silver and the same embroidery edged her modest neckline. Train draped over her arm, she looked like one of the Parthenon Marbles come to life. Ariadne, however, seemed loath to rid herself of her cloak, clutching the black velvet to her chest as she joined her friends.

"Oh, that I might arrive in such style," Daphne said with a sigh.

Oh, that Lord Robert might arrive at all!

Acantha Dalrymple made nearly as good an entrance. She didn't have a deerhound or an ebony sedan chair, but her gown was a gossamer white, with diamond chips that caught the light and made her look as if she'd just stepped from a rainbow. She minced past them with only a sidelong look out of the corners of her eyes, apparently making sure they had seen her.

"As if we could miss her," Ariadne said, lips tight.

Emily shook her head. "I shall be blind for the next quarter hour after forcing my eyes to gaze upon such brilliance."

Daphne giggled. Ariadne peered around her sister. "Oh, good. Mother's gone in. Give me a moment to dispose of my cloak."

Emily frowned. Daphne looked nearly as perplexed, then she clapped one hand over her mouth as Ariadne returned.

Emily was speechless. Gone were the soft pastels, the snowy white silk Lady Rollings so admired. Ariadne's gown was of watered silk in a vivid emerald green that turned her eyes to turquoise. The scalloped neckline drew down over her bosom, and the tiny bodice called attention to every curve. Medallions of black lace decorated the full skirt and edged the short puffy sleeves. Even her gloves and slippers were a sophisticated black.

"Where did you get that?" Daphne demanded.

Ariadne fluffed up her sleeves where the material had been squashed against her cloak. "I saved my pennies and commissioned it. I told you I refused to wear white again."

"Mother will have an apoplectic fit," Daphne predicted. "And I do not care to hear what Lord Snedley has to say." She stood on tiptoe again to peer over the crowd. "Has he arrived?"

"Hang Lord Snedley," Ariadne said, as if the new gown had made her reckless. She linked arms with Emily and Daphne. "We have a criminal to catch. Let's see what waits for us inside and plot the perfect place to confront him with his sins."

"How many places are there in a ballroom?" Emily asked with a frown as she followed Ariadne inside.

As it turned out, entirely too many.

Just as Priscilla had planned, the vast ballroom had been transformed into an enchanted garden. Crimson roses woven into evergreen swags draped the tall columns, perfume scenting the air. Among them nestled gilded cages where bright butterflies fluttered, and statues of creamy marble in Grecian gowns and classic poses dotted the space. A fountain of scarlet punch bubbled in one corner, surrounded by roses and potted ferns, and the musicians of a small orchestra were even now taking their places on the raised platform. On either side of the door to the veranda, great blocks of crystalline ice had been sculpted to look like distant mountains, beckoning the guests. Already the space was filling, color blending with movement, voices blending in welcome, excitement.

Why did Emily have to spend her time hunting Lord Robert?!

Daphne seemed to have the same thought. She tugged them around the room, exclaiming over each new delight. Tall potted evergreens and vines with red-throated flowers the size of dinner plates had been brought in and arranged in the corner.

"It's a maze!" Daphne cried, watching as a couple darted

inside, laughing. As if to decry the fun, from deep within the curtain of green came a horrid shriek that split the cool air and raised goose flesh all along Emily's arms.

"White peacock," Ariadne explained. "Priscilla had me rent a dozen to parade the grounds. One must have gotten loose."

"Either that or the deerhound's found it," Daphne said, staring at the wall of green.

Not far from it lay a hermit's grotto. A stream trickled down a tower of rocks through ferns and roses until it emptied into a small pool. Emily spotted gold moving under the water lilies.

"She had to have goldfish," Ariadne said with a shake of her head.

"And a hermit," Daphne said, nodding to the rugged-looking gentleman seated beside the stream. His battered hat was pulled down low over his stubbled face, and his feet sticking out from under the tattered pants were bare. "Just like at a stately park. The poet Lord Byron would approve."

"'There is society, where none intrudes,'" Ariadne quoted. "By the deep sea, and music in its roar. I love not man the less but Nature more.'"

Priscilla clearly had hired the fellow to portray the man in love with nature, but he seemed a bit too interested in the people around him. Emily shivered, feeling his gaze on them as they headed for the sofas and chairs grouped around the dance floor.

The older ladies and gentlemen had already taken up residence upon the velvet cushions, plumping the pillows behind them.

Lady Wakenoak was not among the group. Had she not come? Had Lord Robert used her absence as an excuse to stay home?

Would Emily never be free of the fellow?

She wanted to scream like the peacock. She felt just as trapped. All her efforts, all her plans, were in vain if Lord Robert did not arrive. But she caught sight of neither he nor Jamie before a servant in glittering white livery shut the double doors to the entryway and Priscilla and her parents turned to their waiting guests.

"That's all right," Ariadne murmured. "He'll simply be fashionably late. That's the perfect trait for a villain."

It certainly was. Emily could not imagine a more potent way of torturing someone.

At the top of the room, Mr. Tate waved a hand. "Welcome to you all! I can only say how proud I am to have reached this moment in our dear daughter's life."

Mrs. Tate wailed and bowed her head, shoulders shaking.

"Allow me, Father," Priscilla said, leaving her father to pat his overcome wife awkwardly on the shoulder of her gown, the front of which was turning a darker hue from her tears.

Priscilla spread her arms as if she longed to hug each guest to her heart. "Welcome, dear friends, beloved family! We are so delighted you could join us tonight. Let our enchanted garden be yours." She clapped her hands.

And a few of the statues woke, stretched, waved white arms gracefully before falling back into new positions.

The guests applauded.

"Thespians," Ariadne said. "From Drury Lane."

"Before we begin the dancing," Priscilla continued, "my dear friend Lady Emily Southwell has a gift for her father, the Duke of Emerson. You'll find it near the entrance."

Near the entrance? Emily had been so concerned about finding Lord Robert that she'd completely forgotten her painting! She'd had Warburton deliver it only this afternoon. As the guests began moving in that direction, Emily hurried past them to reach it first. Her father was already waiting beside it, gazing at it. She could not tell what he was thinking, was afraid to ask. Priscilla had followed her, and the Tates were close behind. Mrs. Tate sniffed back a sob as if she thought something dreadful was going to happen.

Emily certainly hoped she was wrong.

But her entire body started to tremble as everyone stared at the painting. What did they think? What would they say? When others had criticized her battle scenes, she'd risen immediately to the defense. If they criticized this piece, she thought she might crumble into dust.

For from out of the painting, her mother gazed with dark eyes. Her black hair was pulled back from her narrow face, and no one but Emily knew how frizzy it could be in the rain. She was wearing a white gown with a green sash, the Emerson colors, and the smile on her face welcomed everyone she saw. It said she had never met a stranger and never parted from a friend. It said she believed herself with them even now.

A tear ran down Emily's face, but she didn't wipe it away. It felt right, and she knew her mother would understand.

Certainly her father did. His hand came to rest on her shoulder. "You've captured that quality she had that drew me to her from the first. Well done, daughter. This is the greatest gift you could have given me."

Emily's heart was so full, she felt it pressing against the bodice of her mother's beautiful gown. "Thank you, Father."

She chanced a glance around and found everyone gazing at her mother. More than one eye glittered with tears. Priscilla's lips were trembling, and Daphne and Ariadne were wiping at their cheeks. Even the hermit was staring at the piece. Emily'd touched their hearts, and her own swelled to bursting. They were so hushed, she could hear the sound of a clock chiming the hour outside. She did not need to hear each beat to know the time.

It was nine, and Jamie had not come.

Another tear fell, but this one she wiped away as Lady St. Gregory glided to her side. Once more the sculptress was gowned in blue, this time of a cool hue that matched the ice sculptures melting behind her. "An interesting piece, Lady Emily. Not your usual style."

"Indeed no," Acantha Dalrymple said, pushing her way to the front as well. "Perhaps if you'd tried something like this, you might not have lost the Barnsley Prize in Art to me." She smiled winningly at Lady St. Gregory. "And may I say, your ladyship, that I am a great admirer of your work."

A swath of purple caught Emily's eye. Lady Wakenoak had arrived at last. She was standing at the edge of the crowd, an ostrich plume waving over her gray curls.

"Excuse me," Emily murmured, leaving Acantha to toady up to the sculptress to her heart's content.

Lady Wakenoak surprised Emily with a kiss on one cheek. "Lord Robert is here, the naughty boy," she murmured in Emily's ear. "I can't remember where he told me to have you meet him, so you'll simply have to find him."

Find him? Emily straightened away from her with a frown. What game was this? Why didn't he approach her? Did he know she had something planned? Had he outmaneuvered her yet again?

Robert's mother evidently had no such concerns, for she bustled away. Emily turned to follow her and found the hermit standing there. He ducked his head when she looked at him, but for a moment she thought he meant to speak to her.

"Return to your cell," Priscilla scolded, hurrying up to them. "Honestly. What kind of hermit wanders about ballrooms?"

As he slunk back to his corner, Priscilla turned to Emily. "We're about to start the dancing. Has Lord Robert arrived?"

Emily nodded. "Yes. I just have to find him."

"I'd help, but I must start the set. Sorry!" She darted off in search of her partner. Emily didn't dare follow.

Lord Robert was here, somewhere, likely watching her. She had to coax him out among the other guests, then bring him and Lady Skelcroft face to face. For once Emily told the lady that her precious brooch was nothing but a paste copy, Lady Skelcroft was sure to put two and two together and realize that Lord Robert had stolen the original. Her scream of fury would drown out even the lilting melodies from the talented orchestra, bringing all the guests rushing to her side.

If Lady Skelcroft was too dim to take the hint, Emily would be happy to elaborate how Lord Robert had wormed his way into the lady's confidence so he could steal her brooch. He'd only attended Lady Skelcroft's ball to return the paste copy. And if the lady refused to believe Emily's story, Emily was quite ready to unpin the brooch and fling it to the floor. Diamonds did not break against hardwood, but paste did.

Any way Emily looked at it, she would have proven to the world that Lord Robert was a scoundrel. She simply had to put her plan into effect.

Before something dreadful truly did happen.

✦23✦

Jewel Thieves
Prefer the Night

Emily stood by the dance floor, watching even as she felt watched. Priscilla moved confidently through the graceful turns, smiling so winningly that her partner, the elder son of Lord Fishborne, missed his cue watching her and stumbled. Daphne was more stilted, as if she feared it improper to show exuberance. Acantha Dalrymple was grace personified. It wasn't fair.

Still, Emily could not ignore the feeling that she was being carefully observed—even hunted. She glanced around, but no gaze met hers among the courtly guests. Where was Lord Robert? Not among the dancers. Nor could she spot him by the sofas. The hermit was surrounded by giggling ladies; more laughter came from the maze. Wait—was that a russet head by the buffet? Her heartbeat was as unsteady as her steps as she started forward.

Suddenly, the door to the kitchens opened, and out danced a group of children dressed like fairies in fluttering gowns, with gossamer wings on their backs. They darted across the ballroom, making bows, dipping curtsies, and handing out little packages of comfits. The guests exclaimed in delight.

And Emily lost sight of Lord Robert, if she'd ever had him at all.

This was getting her nowhere! Priscilla was the only one who might guess where a gentleman would hide. As the second dance ended, Emily parted the beaus besieging her friend and begged a moment.

"Of *course*," Priscilla said, then clapped her hands again, prompting the statues to twist into more elaborate poses. One looked a bit like a braided bun.

Before Emily could get in another word, a gentleman pushed his way forward. He had brown hair and was only of average height, but his gaze was keen and bright behind his spectacles. He inclined his head to Emily before turning to Priscilla.

"I doubt you remember me, Miss Tate," he said. "We met at Lady Baminger's musicale when you were in town last Christmas. I'm Nathan Kent."

Emily had no time for such interruptions, but Priscilla smiled politely. "A pleasure to see you again, Mr. Kent." Her gaze returned to Emily, as if she had already dismissed him from her thoughts.

But the gentleman was entirely too persistent. "Forgive the interruption," he continued with another smile to Emily, "but I came to beseech a favor."

He was doomed. Mr. Kent was simply not handsome enough to capture Priscilla's attention. She tossed her curls and gave him her very best "you'd be wise to go away" stare.

Until he added, "For my employer, the Duke of Rottenford."

Priscilla's jaw dropped, and Emily felt her own doom approaching. It wouldn't matter what she said. She would never get Priscilla's attention now!

"The Duke of Rottenford?" Priscilla asked, voice trembling.

"Yes, Rottenford," Mr. Kent agreed with an amused smile. "I serve as his personal secretary."

"Priscilla," Emily tried without much hope.

Priscilla fluttered her lashes and laid a hand on the arm of Mr. Kent's black evening coat. "I would do anything for His Grace."

Mr. Kent detached her hand from his arm. "Then tell me the way through the maze. It's blocking the stairs to the retiring rooms and, after six glasses of your excellent punch, it's become rather urgent, I'm afraid, for His Grace to find his way through."

Priscilla's smile remained on her face, disguising the immense disappointment she must have felt that His Grace was not requesting a dance. "I'd be delighted to tell His Grace, but I cannot spoil the fun for my other guests. If you'd bring him to me, I'll whisper it in his ear."

Oh, but she was cunning. Just what Emily needed!

"Alas," Mr. Kent said with a bit of humor in his voice, crossing the room to your side might pose a difficulty. Perhaps you'd be so kind as to whisper it in *my* ear."

"No, Miss Tate," another young man nearby called. "Whisper it in my ear, and I'll be happy to tell His Grace for you."

They all jostled to get closer, and Priscilla held up a hand. "Gentlemen, gentlemen. We must have mercy. Mr. Kent?"

Mr. Kent eyed Priscilla as if expecting some trap, but he leaned closer. Priscilla pressed her lips to his ear and murmured low. He straightened and walked away, his steps decidedly crooked. But what amazed Emily was the dreamy smile that played upon Priscilla's face!

"Help me find Lord Robert!" Emily demanded.

"Who?" Priscilla asked, blinking.

Emily groaned and gave up. When she needed action, she should have known who to ask. She dodged around the dance floor once more and finally located Daphne and Ariadne near the far wall. Daphne was deep in conversation with an elderly gentleman, her train over one arm.

"*Excuse* us," Emily said, seizing their arms and dragging them to the side. "I need your help to find Lord Robert."

"Of course," Daphne said. "I was merely trying to find Lord Snedley. He's here somewhere! My night will not be complete unless he pronounces me a success."

Ariadne rolled her eyes.

"Once I deal with Lord Robert, I'll be happy to help you find him," Emily promised.

They started about the circuit again, peering around, under, and over everyone they saw. Ariadne kept silent, one hand around her waist. It seemed even her emerald gown had not emboldened her to converse with strangers. Not even to the deerhound lady.

"Gorgeous gown, my dear," she said to Ariadne as they paused near her. The beast at her side turned his golden gaze on Ariadne as if wondering how long it would take to run her down. His mistress held out the chain to Ariadne. "Be a love and hold my pet while I find my partner to dance."

Ariadne gasped, but she could not protest quickly enough as the lady pressed the leash into her hand.

"Actually," Emily tried, nudging Ariadne, "we were trying to find Lord Robert Townsend, my fiancé."

"Look in Lady Skelcroft's circle," the lady advised as she sailed onto the floor. The deerhound and Ariadne regarded each other, the beast's head level with Ariadne's chin. Only the deerhound looked amused.

"Go on," Ariadne said, so still she might have been frozen in place. "Find Lord Robert. I'll be all right. Very likely the creature is trained."

"I could stay," Daphne volunteered, but Ariadne shook her head.

"You'll be of more help to Emily. *You* can talk to people."

In the end, Emily and Daphne left her and hurried for the dowagers' circle, not far from the hermit's grotto. Lady Skelcroft sat among the silver- and gray-haired ladies, complaining, as usual.

Emily dipped a curtsy in front of her. "Pardon me, but I'm trying to find my fiancé, Lord Robert Townsend."

Lady Skelcroft clutched her lace shawl closer, the brooch flashing. "Why come to me, then? I'm not his keeper."

"Not recently," another woman said. The rest laughed behind their fans.

Lady Skelcroft drew herself up haughtily but spoiled it by sneezing three times. "Bother these plants! Whatever possessed Miss Tate to drag in the entire countryside?"

"I believe she was trying to portray an enchanted garden," Daphne said helpfully. "Gardens do have plants."

"Be that as it may," Emily tried, "I would appreciate any word you might have of Lord Robert's whereabouts."

Lady Skelcroft opened her mouth, and Emily cringed to hear what would come out. But the lady sneezed again, in violent bursts. Her hair flew off, landing in a heap on the polished floor.

Everyone stared at it. The black curls lay spread like a bloated spider. Emily swore they even twitched. Her gaze jerked back up and met Lady Skelcroft's. The woman's gray eyes were round, as was her very bald head.

"You stupid girl!" She leapt to her feet, snatched up the wig, and crammed it back on her head. With the curls dangling in disarray, she ran for the maze and disappeared inside.

"My, that was a surprise," Daphne said.

No, that was a tragedy. With Lady Skelcroft in hiding, how was Emily to prove her brooch false?

"Go after her," she told Daphne. "I'll find Lord Robert."

She circled the room yet again, growing more concerned each moment. Where was Lord Robert? How had he disappeared so well?

Where was Jamie? Had she so demeaned herself in his eyes that he could not bear to keep his promise and come?

Priscilla met her beside the dance floor. "Sorry, Emily, but this is not going as I'd planned. Rottenford is lost in the maze, despite my precise instructions, and I have no idea when he'll escape. I'd find him, but I'm supposed to be the hostess!"

She clapped her hands. The statues twisted about again, and two ended up on their rears. "Oh, for pity's sake!"

Daphne hurried up as well. "The night's a disaster! Lady Skelcroft won't come out. And no one will admit to being Lord Snedley."

Ariadne puffed up. "I'm exhausted of looking after that dog! And I go to all the trouble of procuring a decent gown, and I still cannot find a single word to say to a gentleman!"

"Lord Snedley advises letting the young man initiate the conversation," Daphne lectured her sister. "And to keep the topics to the weather, your horses, and your grandmother's snuff recipe."

"*Lord Snedley*," Ariadne said through clenched teeth, "will not help me now."

Daphne shook her head. "Lord Snedley knows a great deal, like Mother. You should read him. You read everything else."

"I don't need to read Lord Snedley," Ariadne grit out.

Daphne sucked in a breath and let it out forcefully, as if trying to keep her patience. "You can be the most stubborn person! There's nothing wrong with taking advice, especially from someone as learned and experienced as Lord Snedley."

"He isn't a saint, you know," Ariadne argued, her color rising.

"Well, he's certainly a lot wiser than you," Daphne countered.

Emily exchanged glances with Priscilla and knew they were both wondering how to intervene.

Ariadne put both hands on her hips. "The fellow's ridiculous. And *you're* ridiculous for caring so much what he thinks!"

"You take that back," Daphne demanded. "You know nothing about him."

"Yes I do!" Ariadne snapped. "I *am* Lord Snedley!"

Emily stared, and Daphne turned as white as the statues.

Priscilla rubbed her ear. "I am truly going mad tonight. I thought you said you're Lord Snedley."

"I am," Ariadne insisted. "I wanted to dress well for the ball, and my allowance wasn't enough for a gown. I may not be able to speak my mind, but I can certainly write. So I gathered up all Mother's platitudes into an etiquette book. I was afraid no publisher would take me seriously, so Lord Snedley was born."

Ariadne turned to her sister. "I never thought he'd go over so well, or that you'd become a devotee. I'm sorry I didn't tell you. I just wanted to be myself for once, with a gown I liked, and writing the etiquette book was the only way I knew."

Daphne stared at her, jaw clenched, then turned and stalked off, heading for the maze. Deep inside it came another high-pitched shriek.

"Is that the peacock or one of my guests?" Priscilla asked with a frown. "I simply cannot tell the difference."

Ariadne sighed. "Daphne had such high hopes for tonight. I've ruined it for her, haven't I?"

"Nonsense," Emily said. "We'll speak to her. But please, you must help me. I've looked everywhere, and I can't find Lord Robert."

Ariadne frowned. "Have you tried the veranda?"

The veranda? Why would he be on the veranda? Emily needed him in the ballroom, where she could accuse him before witnesses. Where Jamie, when he arrived, could see that she knew Robert for what he was. Where she could hand him to Jamie and say, "Arrest him, my love." That is, if Jamie ever showed up.

Well, if Lord Robert was on the veranda, she'd simply have to lure him back inside. "I'll look," she said to Ariadne. "Perhaps you should rescue Daphne from the peacock."

"Or vice versa," Ariadne agreed, hurrying away.

Emily slipped outside. Moonlight shone on the stone terrace, frosting the plants below with silver. Another white peacock strutted past, like a dandy's ghost in his finery.

"Good evening, Emily," Lord Robert said, moving out of the shadows. "It's about time you showed up."

Her heart began to pound as he walked toward her. Out of habit, her hand came up to her chest for her locket and met the hard stones of the emeralds. She'd finally discovered him, yet she found herself completely unprepared for the confrontation.

"Robert, you startled me," she said, hoping he would take her breathlessness as nothing more.

"How very bad of me," he said. He didn't sound the least bit sorry. "Walk with me and let me apologize."

With him in this strange mood, she didn't dare. "Come back inside with me," she tried, "and you can apologize there."

"Ah, no," he said. "Jewel thieves prefer the night."

Something was wrong. He shouldn't be confessing. She was supposed to surprise him with the truth. She edged away from him along the balustrade, feeling the stones snag on her gloves. "A jewel thief?" she asked.

"Oh, come now, Emily. You know I stole Acantha Dalrymple's pearls and Lady Skelcroft's brooch and replaced the stones with paste so no one would be any wiser. Is taking a few jewels so wicked? Miss Dalrymple and Lady Skelcroft won't miss them."

So, she had been right. If she agreed now, would he let her get away? He was watching her every movement; Emily could see her gown outlined in the dark of his eyes. She took a step toward him, ready to bolt. "And what of Lavinia Haversham? Her family is not so fortunate."

His face twisted. "They should be honored I would even notice their daughter. What were a few baubles compared with acceptance in Good Society? But would she be silent when she caught me with my hand in her jewel case? Oh, no."

The emeralds felt as tight as a noose. Emily could not move. "Oh, God. You killed her!"

"It was an accident," Robert spat out. "I struck her once, to keep her quiet. I can't help it if the stupid chit fell into the sharp point of the dressing table. I was lucky to escape before anyone knew I'd been higher than the sitting room."

"You'll hang," Emily said, gathering her wits. If she ran, would he catch her? If she could get past him, she knew help was waiting inside. Surely he'd do nothing before witnesses. "If I were you, I'd take ship for the Continent, tonight."

He drew himself up. "Are you mad? I'm a Townsend. I have a reputation to protect. Besides, the only one who suspects anything is that bastard Cropper. And you." He lunged for her.

"Priscilla!" Emily cried, darting around him for the door. "Ariadne! Daphne! Help!"

One hand came down on her shoulder, jerking her to a stop and slamming her back against him. The other hand came over her mouth, pressing her lips back against her teeth. She could taste the silk of his glove.

"Silence!" His shake rattled her bones.

Never! She wiggled against him, turning her head this way and that, but his grip was too sure, his arms too strong. He dragged her toward the stairs to the garden below.

"I heard what Cropper said to you that night at dinner," he said against her hair. "I already suspected you conspired against me. So I thought I'd let you have your ball. Let everyone see you cavorting with Cropper. Only Mother knew I was here, and she'd never speak a word against me. And when you were found dead in the garden and the emeralds missing, Cropper would be blamed. After all, Good Society would hardly accuse one of their own. Why even your father must have heard me say I'd blame Cropper if anything happened to you. Any accusations from Cropper against me would be taken as the ravings of a desperate criminal. And I would play the grieving lover."

He gave her another shake. "As if I would grieve for you."

Panic crushed the breath from her, made her heart jerk in her chest, threatened to swamp all reason. No, no, she could not give in to it. Robert didn't know Jamie hadn't come. He'd kill her, and no one would know what had happened.

She had to do something. As Lord Robert started down the stairs, she wedged a leg between his.

He stumbled, and for a moment she thought she'd killed them both. Cursing, he righted himself, but she could feel his hold slipping. She sank her teeth into his hand.

He jerked away from her, and she fell onto the ground at the bottom of the stone steps, landing on both feet with her gown beneath her. She ran anyway, pulling it up as she moved, dragging the silk through the graveled path. Her only coherent thought was that she mustn't damage her gown or Priscilla would kill her.

If Lord Robert didn't catch her first.

24

Three Meanings of the Letter "L"

Emily dodged behind a shrub and gasped for breath. Why did her gown have to be white? The pearly color glowed in the moonlight, like a beacon guiding sailors to harbor.

Or a murderer to his victim.

She could hear Lord Robert blundering through the bushes, curses tainting his breath.

"Do not make me hunt you down," he called in warning. "It will go worse for you."

Worse? He was going to kill her anyway. Like the soldiers in her paintings, she must face the fact that she might meet her Maker. *Please, Lord, not until I tell Jamie I love him!*

The scent of cloves drifted past, much too close. Emily whipped her head around as she tried to find him before he found her. Was that dark shape Robert? No, another shrub. That snap, his foot on a twig, or her own? She crouched lower, scrunched her skirts together, ready to flee at the least movement.

"Lady Emily!"

Jamie's voice was like a rope reaching down to rescue her from a well. Yet she dared not respond, even as other voices joined his. She could hear movement, coming closer. Tears welled up in her eyes, and she held back a thankful sob.

"Not yet, I think," Lord Robert said.

Emily's heart slammed into her chest as he yanked her to her feet. She struggled for purchase in the damp dirt of the garden, but her cry for help was cut off as his hand looped through the gold setting of the emeralds and wrenched it against her neck. Her voice was locked in her throat, her breath in her lungs. She scrambled with her fingers, gloves slipping on the stones, trying to break the hold. She could not let him win!

The clasp broke, and Emily tumbled to the ground, gasping for air. "Here!" she cried, voice rough. "I'm here!"

Feet pounded in all directions. One pair surely belonged to Lord Robert, running away, the coward. She was alone only a second before she was surrounded and lifted to her feet.

"That way," she said, pointing. "He's escaping."

"Not for long," said Mr. Kent. Others joined him, the sound of pursuit fading in the night.

She looked up to find that the hermit was cradling her in his arms. His hat covered most of his face so that all she could see was his smile, and it was positively wicked.

She frowned. "Jamie?"

The smile widened, and she hugged him to her. The wool of his coat was rough and warm against her cheek. The night air was less cool with his arms around her. She fancied she could hear his heart beating as quickly as her own, but that truly must have been a fancy, for she knew he could not care for her. Could he?

"Emily?"

Jamie released her at the sound of her father's voice. Priscilla, Daphne, and Ariadne crowded around her father, all looking frightfully worried, along with Viscount Rollings, Acantha Dalrymple, several men she'd met at the engagement dinner, a statue, and the flock of fairies, one missing a wing.

"Lady Emily is safe," Jamie reported, handing her to her father as if his job was done. She'd helped him catch a criminal, and now he'd be off on his next investigation, her face, her person forgotten. She wanted to hide under the bush.

"I regret, however," Jamie continued, "that Lord Robert has escaped with the emeralds."

His Grace frowned as a murmur ran through the group.

"No, he hasn't," Emily said. "Those were paste copies. I sent the originals north to Cousin Charles and Helena yesterday."

Her father gazed down at her with a shake of his head. "Well done. But you might have told me what you were about."

"I had no proof Lord Robert was a jewel thief, Father, but I knew he'd stolen Lady Skelcroft's brooch and Miss Dalrymple's pearls. He murdered Miss Haversham when she caught him. He only agreed to marry me to deflect suspicion, until he learned I suspected him as well. Tonight he meant to steal the emeralds, kill me, and blame it on Mr. Cropper."

More gasps rang out.

"That's silly!" Acantha Dalrymple cried, hand on her pearls. "Lord Robert's no thief. My pearls are right here."

"No, they aren't," Daphne said. "Lady Emily is telling the

truth. I heard Lord Robert confess."

Now Emily frowned. "You did?"

Daphne nodded. "I heard voices so I crawled out on the ledge by the ladies' retiring room."

"You could have been killed!" a statue cried.

"Not really," Daphne said. "I dragged the commode to the window and tied my train to it as an anchor. And I saw the entire scene. Besides, someone had to protect Lady Emily, and I have the most skill."

"Dear God," her father muttered. "Don't tell your mother."

"And when I got stuck coming back through the maze to tell everyone," Daphne continued blissfully, "Priscilla chopped down a portion with a chair. And Ariadne climbed onstage and blew the ophicleide to get everyone's attention, then explained that you were in danger. And then Mr. Cropper revealed himself and took charge, and we knew everything would be fine. And it was."

"It most certainly was not!" Acantha Dalrymple exclaimed. "Your escapades will be on everyone's tongues! I might have known you four couldn't put on a proper ball."

"On the contrary," Emily said, linking arms with Priscilla, Daphne, and Ariadne. "We've just given the event of the Season. But you are right about one thing. This night will be the talk of London, especially the part about your pearls being nothing but paste."

"I wonder," Priscilla put in with a smile, "if other parts of her are too?"

As Acantha gasped and clutched her bosom, La Petite Four headed back to the ballroom and to the wonders of the night they had worked so hard to achieve.

And so the ball was the huge success Priscilla had wanted, if not, precisely, for the same reasons. Mr. Kent returned to tell His Grace that Lord Robert had been caught and taken to Newgate Prison. It did not quite seem real to Emily as she promenaded about the Elysium Assembly Rooms with the others. People she'd only just met smiled at her, waved to her from across the room. Rumors had circulated that something had happened, and they were the heroines of the piece. Some enterprising young person had even learned their sobriquet and shared it with the guests.

"So now all of London knows we are La Petite Four," Ariadne said proudly. "No doubt they think we earned the name because we are so sweet."

"I would not call you sweet," Daphne said. "Not after the way you let me prattle on about Lord Snedley."

Ariadne hung her head.

Daphne draped her arm around her bare shoulders. "I should have known it was the work of my brilliant sister."

Ariadne raised her head with a smile, and all knew she had been forgiven.

Emily had her own confession to make. When she'd been alone in the garden, she'd sworn the night would not end before she confessed her feelings for Jamie. She turned to look for him and found herself facing Lady St. Gregory.

"A most interesting night, Lady Emily," she said in her usual cool tone. "You are quite a singular young lady."

Was that praise? Emily could not believe it. "Thank you, your ladyship," she said politely.

"I wish to speak with you about the portrait of your mother. Was that difficult?"

Why did Lady St. Gregory ask such questions? Emily never knew how to answer. "It was the easiest and hardest piece I've ever done," she admitted. "The colors, her face, they came easily. Conveying the person I loved was very, very hard."

Lady St. Gregory smiled. "Yet you did it. I never met your mother, but looking at the painting, I fancy I know her, and you. I imagine she'd be very, very proud of you."

Emily blinked back tears. "Thank you, your ladyship."

Lady St. Gregory inclined her head. "I give praise where it is due. I believe we have room for an artist of your caliber in the Royal Society for the Beaux Arts. What do you say?"

Emily stared at her. Then, seeing the truth in the woman's broad smile, she broke into a grin herself. "I say thank you very much, your ladyship. Thank you very much indeed!"

Her delight lasted only as long as it took for Lady St. Gregory to give her the particulars of the next meeting. Then her stomach began to squirm again. Her gaze swept the room, searching. Priscilla was on the dance floor with a tall, bucktoothed fellow Emily could only guess was the mighty Duke of Rottenford.

Beyond them, Ariadne had cornered the famous playwright Mr. Sheridan and was happily quizzing him on his life in the theatre. Not far away, Daphne was chatting with several fellows, all of whom seemed quite impressed by a lady who could climb out a window and perch on a ledge in her ball gown.

But then Emily saw him, standing by the doors to the veranda. The glow from the beeswax candles in the crystal chandeliers overhead glinted off his russet hair.

Jamie caught her gaze on him and raised two fingers to his forehead. Then he disappeared out onto the veranda.

Emily followed.

He was waiting in the moonlight. "Everything all right, then?"

Not in the slightest, but she nodded. "Yes. I suppose you'll be off to the next case."

He shrugged. "Such is the life of a Runner. You understand now why I couldn't tell you that I was investigating Lord Robert. Mr. Haversham contacted Bow Street after he found that his daughter's jewels had been converted to paste. When the Marquess of Skelcroft complained about his wife's brooch going missing, only to have it reappear as paste, I saw that the only connection between the two cases was Lord Robert Townsend."

Emily nodded again. Where were her good intentions? She wanted to stand here, drinking in the sight of him, talking to him about anything, everything. "So you came in disguise tonight hoping to catch him."

"In part," he said. "But in truth, I had to come."

Emily made a face. "I suppose I did sound rather cryptic in my note. I didn't want to tell you that I planned to expose Lord Robert. I wanted you to see it, to know that I . . ."

He strode to her side and took her hands in his. "You what, Lady Emily?"

She couldn't say it, couldn't risk it. Not when she was certain he had no feelings for her besides a reluctant admiration. Or did he? He had given her one clue. Perhaps she should do some investigating of her own.

"I wanted to know what you meant by your note about the ball," she said. "There was the little matter of an L."

"An L?" He sounded surprised.

"An L," she insisted. "Just before your initials. I could not determine what it meant."

He was quiet for a moment, which she knew meant he was choosing his words with care. Finally, he said, "Most people would take it as a time notation, placed as it was next to the nine. L for later."

"Ah," she said, feeling foolish. "Of course." Was it too late to crawl away and cry?

"A few, however," he continued, a smile in his voice, "might take it as a description. L for longingly."

"Oh," she said, her heartbeat speeding.

"And the bold ones," he finished, leaning closer and lowering his voice, "might take it one step further. Let's say, L for lovingly."

Emily swallowed. "I've been known to be bold."

"I would have wagered my life on it. And that's why I had to come to the ball, Emily. I had to tell you that I love you. The other night, at the dinner party when I thought I'd lost you to Lord Robert, I lashed out. I'm sorry."

"You had a right," she protested. "I hadn't realized that I was using you. I just wanted to catch him so badly."

"I know that now. Tonight, when I saw the painting of your mother, I knew you couldn't love someone like Lord Robert. Yet I nearly lost you to him again."

Inside, the musicians struck up a waltz. The sound floated over them, lilting. Her heart floated right along with it.

"You couldn't lose me, Jamie. I love you too."

His smile captured her heart and held it gently. "Dance with me?"

She nodded, too full of joy to speak. He wrapped one hand around hers and rested the other above her waist, holding her in his embrace. Emily's hand trembled as she placed it on his broad shoulder. His gaze met hers, solemn.

And they began to move in time to the music, backward, forward, turn. She knew the steps. The last time she'd practiced them, she'd been partnering Daphne.

This was nothing like partnering Daphne.

His touch was sure, his steps smooth. She was constantly aware of how close he was, how near their bodies. His arm brushed her chest as they moved; her cheek grazed his as they turned. With his gaze on hers, she felt more beautiful than Priscilla, more graceful than Daphne on horseback, as brilliant as

Ariadne. She knew there was nothing she couldn't do.

Emily never wanted the music to stop, but stop it did. His steps slowed, and she slowed as well, sliding her hand down his strong arm. He caught it and brought both of her hands to his chest, tender, reverent. Mesmerized, she willed him to bend closer, to bridge the distance between his lips and hers.

And he did.

She closed her eyes, let herself feel the sweet pressure. Time seemed to stop, to stretch. When he drew back, he sounded as breathless as she felt.

"You should go in," he murmured with a touch to her cheek. "They'll all be looking for you."

She didn't want to go, not now, not ever. She just wanted to be here with him. But that couldn't be. He was right. She had responsibilities, duties, the Royal Society to join, an entire Season to enjoy.

"When will I see you again?" she asked, suddenly afraid.

His smile was a promise. "Soon."

She smiled back. "Then, until later, Jamie."

He grinned. "Until later, Emily."

She held his hand a moment longer, then stepped away from him to return to the ball. Surely there would be other dances, other kisses with the man she loved. Some might even be better than this.

She could only dream.

❖ *The End* ❖